The passage was dark . . .

Dorcas passed the door of the study and the door of the laundry chute. She passed the telephone room.

Or rather she did not pass it.

For her foot struck something soft and yielding. The rug rolled up, a coat dropped, she thought and looked down.

The thing on the floor was dim and white and it was a man's hand.

She must have pulled open the door to the telephone room. For now it was open and, huddled awkwardly, half in and half out of the little room, was a black lump that was completely sodden and inert.

It was the man whose hand she had almost trod with her foot.

She said something and put her hand upon him and jerked it instantly, sharply, away.

The fingers were wet and dark and Dorcas screamed.

"Love, mystery, and detection woven into an ingenious tale whose tension remains on a high level to the end. Capital."

—*Saturday Review*

MIGNON G. EBERHART
HASTY WEDDING

WARNER BOOKS

A Warner Communications Company

Dedication:

To
ALAN
Who still listens

All the persons and events in this book are entirely imaginary. Nothing in it is derived from anything which ever happened.

THE AUTHOR.

WARNER BOOKS EDITION

Copyright 1937, 1938 by Mignon G. Eberhart
Copyright renewed
© 1965, 1966 by Mignon G. Eberhart
All rights reserved.

This Warner Books Edition is published by arrangement with the author.

Warner Books, Inc.
666 Fifth Avenue
New York, N.Y. 10103

 A Warner Communications Company

Printed in the United States of America

First Warner Books Printing: April, 1985

Reissued: October, 1988

10 9 8 7 6 5 4 3

CHAPTER 1

HER OWN IMAGE advanced and retreated in the distant pier glass.

"Slower," said Sophie. "Stop. . . . Now turn again."

"This way, if you please, Miss Whipple," said the fitter.

That was in March.

In January Dorcas Whipple, with her mother and Sophie in Miami Beach, was all but engaged to Ronald. In February her mother roused to the state of affairs, came home to Chicago and rallied all her cohorts. On March eleventh Dorcas stood before the mirror and looked at herself in her wedding gown, mistily through the white veil, and the image it gave back to her was unreal and ethereal in quality—as Dorcas herself was not.

It was the final and last fitting. The wedding was at noon the next day and the man she was marrying was not Ronald Drew.

She hadn't been really desperately unhappy, she thought, listening absently to the fitter and Sophie, who were rapidly reaching a point of agreement.

She had defended Ronald hotly all the way through the thing; had fought for him with increased zeal because they were all against him. Had given in finally because the proofs had to be admitted, because she could not fight against her mother's weapons, because after all, as was pointed out to her, she was twenty-four, she had known the man she was to marry all her life, it was an eminently suitable marriage and it was time she married and took over her rightful responsibilities.

What Cary Whipple hadn't said was that she wanted her daughter to be married and settled before she died but it didn't need saying, for Cary's gentleness and semi-invalidism said it for her. Only once had she come near bringing her strongest weapon into use and that was when she looked at Dorcas with her soft blue eyes and said: "I'm stronger than I look, my dear. I wouldn't want you to hurry into marriage simply because it would be a satisfaction to me—it may be years yet."

5

She had said no more. But it had actually, Dorcas supposed, decided the thing.

But even after her engagement had been announced Dorcas had to admit in all honesty she was not really terribly unhappy. Not, at least, until—well, when had thoughts of Ronald begun to haunt her so constantly? Just lately? When the marriage was, all at once, so near and so completely inevitable?

She looked at the slender white figure in the huge old pier glass and it seemed to look back at her enigmatically through the white veil. It was as if that distant reflection knew things Dorcas did not know—things about Dorcas Whipple, who was so soon to be Dorcas Locke.

Had she been, she wondered, quite fair to Ronald? The fitter murmured to Sophie.

"Turn again, will you, Dorcas?" said Sophie. "That back panel . . ."

Dorcas pivoted. The mysterious image in the mirror vanished. Opposite her now were windows and a leaden sky and bare, wet brown trees.

It was a dark, gusty day with a raw wind off the lake.

All the way home from rehearsal at St Chrystofer's it had blown fine mist against the windows of the car and along the Drive you could see great, slate-gray waves breaking savagely in white foam against the breakwater. Dorcas had pulled her fur coat tighter about her throat and thought with incredulity of January; hot white sand, golden sun, blue sky and Ronald. They had danced such a lot, she had remembered suddenly, during those dark, tropical nights and Ronald danced as smoothly and gracefully as one of the professional adagio dancers they so often saw together at the casino.

There had been a hundred things to see to at the rehearsal; luckily all arrangements for the wedding had passed through Sophie's capable, lovely hands. Dorcas had been preoccupied with walking with suitably measured tread down the dim church aisle and toward the altar. The bridesmaids had worn their yellow gowns and Dorcas herself, in her plain blue wool street dress had looked, she felt, remarkably unbridelike. And had felt, meeting Jevan Locke before that untenanted altar, suddenly a little frightened, as if, till that moment, she hadn't comprehended the thing she was undertaking. It had made her silent; very cool and sober.

Sally Notten had ruffled her yellow chiffon train and pouted. "Dorcas is as cool as if she'd been married a dozen times. I'm lots more excited than she is right now," and had looked appealingly at Jevan, who only laughed.

Then there had been photographers; were to be, the next morning, more photographers. Sophie's account of the wedding, with all the names clearly and accurately typed, was already in the hands of the city's society editors.

All the way home through the fine, slanting rain and wind and cold Dorcas had thought of Ronald and had fought an increasing sense of panic.

It had become more and more poignant, so by the time they had turned off the South Shore Drive and wound through a gray, desolate park and reached at last, after passing glimpses of a storm-shrouded Midway, their own street, Dorcas was oddly apprehensive. Almost as if some climax, some crisis of which she had been up till then unaware, now threatened her.

They had reached the Whipple house and the car had turned in at the drive.

It was a large, ugly house built long before the North Shore became fashionable and Pennyforth Whipple had remained there along with a few others during the rapid hegira northward of the war period. During the 1920s his widow did not dream of selling the house as so many others did. It was built of red brick, huge and solid, with plate-glass windows and a black slate roof and somber chimneys hovering above it; there was a great deal of wood used in its wide ornamented doors and stairways and the cavernous central hall was paneled in wood. The rooms were large and high ceilinged and there were a great many of them. Pennyforth Whipple must have had a large and increasing family in mind when he built the house and married a young wife, but there was only Dorcas and Cary's semi-invalidism which made her in many ways so like another child to her elderly husband. Yet Cary had been thirty, fragile, and appealing in her gentle fragility, when Dorcas was born. She was now fifty-four and still rather childish and still fragile and gentle. Her eyes had faded a little; her hair was a softly waved gray; her fine skin looked a little powdery and very soft where it had lost some of its firmness. Her small hands, usually jeweled, showed blue veins; her mouth had changed a little in shape where she wore an artificial denture. Otherwise, since the years had treated her kindly, she looked very much as she had looked when Pennyforth Whipple was alive.

People always indulged Cary; always took care of her. Even her money had been left to her as an allowance from Dorcas' fortune in order to protect her. It was a large allowance, fifteen hundred a month, out of which she paid only for her own clothing and charities, gifts and theater tickets. All the household expenses—for the Chicago home and for the Lake Geneva summer place—all the travel expenses, all the taxes and incidentals were paid out of the bulk of her husband's money, which was left in trusteeship for Dorcas.

It had been Pennyforth Whipple's way of protecting Cary against fortune hunters and at the same time of insuring her comfort. It was a wise provision and it relieved Cary of responsibility for a really sizable fortune which thus belonged unconditionally to Dorcas—or would belong to her unconditionally as soon as she married, when the trusteeship would automatically dissolve. That, Dorcas thought dryly, was one of their reasons for wanting her to marry Jevan. He could manage the money. But Ronald hadn't been, as they had openly said at the last, a fortune hunter.

Ronald.

The car had rolled gently under the ornamented porte-cochere and stopped. Rain had whirled gustily against her cheeks as she followed her mother in at the side door.

It had then been about five o'clock and growing dark, so that lights were on here and there.

They had gone along the side hall, past the door of the room that had been Penn Whipple's study and into the main hall, its marquetry floors spacious and darkly glistening where they were not covered with long, thin oriental rugs. There was a bronze boy holding a flowered lamp at the stairway. There was a marble head of a woman—Dorcas had never known just what woman—in a niche beside the door. It was all, probably, in bad taste but it was splendidly, robustly Victorian and achieved a kind of harmony. Cary would have changed nothing. When it was built and furnished it was considered one of the most elegant homes in Chicago. It had, all of it, suited Pennyforth Whipple and the period when it was built and nothing in the Whipple house ever wore out, thus why should it be replaced?

Since Pennyforth Whipple's death the house had been

closed a great deal, for Cary and Dorcas, and usually Sophie, traveled; stopped here and there for Dorcas to go to school, traveled again. They came back at intervals and opened the Chicago house and renewed their social connections. There had been no question but that the wedding should take place there, for Chicago was home. Their dearest, oldest ties were in Chicago. Their best and oldest friends.

A middle-aged maid with a full skirt which came exactly to her ankles had taken Dorcas' coat and told her the wedding dress was ready for the last fitting. It was Sophie who had been dissatisfied with the fit of the sheathlike white satin gown; Sophie who had insisted on a last alteration. Sophie had a flair for clothes; she often took things Dorcas had used, dresses that had proved to be unbecoming, chiffons that had been worn a few times, and made them over for herself and did it, with a little help for the fittings, expertly, because she so loved clothes.

Again Dorcas was vaguely aware that the fitter and Sophie were murmuring and Sophie rose gracefully, unfastened her thin brown stockings and knelt down herself beside Dorcas. "Turn again, Dorcas," she said. "A little more . . . there." Dorcas felt Sophie's expert fingers giving a little tug to her dress, a twist this way and that. A long pause while the fitter, smart in her black gown, and Sophie again scrutinized and murmured.

"Now walk a little, Dorcas. Toward the mirror . . . that's right."

Again a tall white figure, inscrutable, mysterious because of the floating white veil, advanced to meet Dorcas. Tomorrow that figure was to become herself. Were all brides frightened—even brides who were making sensible, well-advised marriages? Brides who were giving up romance? Who were giving up men like Ronald Drew? She wondered again (with again a hovering sense of something curiously like apprehension) whether she had been altogether fair with Ronald. Whether—whether after all she had loved him as deeply as she was ever to love anyone.

She was terribly tired, she told herself abruptly. Absurdly taut and nervous. She wished they would finish the fitting and leave her in peace and quiet.

Almost immediately Sophie, always tactful, said: "That will do now. That's really very nice."

The fitter was anxious, placative, complimentary. She lifted the veil from Dorcas' short brown hair.

"Miss Whipple is a beautiful bride," she said. "It's been a pleasure to work on her things. I hope you'll come to us after your marriage, Miss Whipple."

Dorcas, looking into the reflection of her own face which was clearer now that the veil was removed, thought candidly that she had never looked worse in her life and thanked the woman absently.

Sophie rose lithely, pulled down her girdle and refastened her stockings, showing an expanse of handsome legs. She took off her smart hat, ran her fingers over smooth dark hair and said pleasantly: "It's all right now, I'm sure. That's all, thank you."

The fitter went away, smiling and complimenting and looking with quick side glances at the house, at the heavy old mahogany and thick green curtains; at the incongruous chintz covers; at Dorcas' wide, laden dressing table.

"I'll help you out of the dress," said Sophie. Cary came to the door, looked at her daughter with her lovely soft eyes and went away again.

Dorcas struggled out of the clinging, tight white satin and for a fantastic instant it seemed to be suffocating in its soft weight.

"I'll hang it up," said Sophie. "Here's a warm robe. For heaven's sake, don't catch cold. There's nothing so disgusting as a sniffly bride." She gave Dorcas a tailored flannel house-coat and said unexpectedly: "Are you going to see Ronald again?"

"Ronald! . . . No."

"Oh," said Sophie. "Well, I suppose it's better not to."

Dorcas wrapped the flannel robe around her, kicked off her brown street pumps and leaned back in the chaise longue wearily.

"Of course it's better. That's over. I'll never see him again."

Sophie gave a competent look at some boxes of underclothing yet to be packed and sat down opposite Dorcas, crossing her legs and lighting a cigarette. She was a handsome woman of about forty-five; handsome in a rather delicate and well-bred way with fine bones, a long slim neck from which she fought wrinkles; dark hazel eyes, well made up, and a fine figure. She had been Thomas Whipple's second and younger wife. Tom Whipple was Pennyforth Whipple's brother; he had made and lost at least three fortunes and it was unfortunately during the losing of the third that he had died. Naturally Pennyforth Whipple had taken care of Sophie, settling a generous sum upon her at this death, a sum which was augmented later by an allowance given her by Dorcas.

She had social charm and grace; below that pleasant surface she was worldly and extremely practical. She said now, linking her hands around her knee: "I'll finish packing the last trunk after dinner. They'd better go tonight. I can have them sent about ten. Are there any last odds and ends to go in, Dorcas?"

Tonight.

"There's no hurry," said Dorcas quickly. "Tomorrow morning will be all right——"

"I suppose so. Only there are so many things to see to. I've checked the lists. By the way, I forgot the Bramtons—Cary didn't think of them either. Awful, wasn't it? I called up and lied myself black, saying the invitation must have got lost. Well, my dear, this time tomorrow you'll be married and gone and the thing will be over."

Ronald, thought Dorcas. What would he be doing then? Would he be thinking of her, needing her? He loved her; she had never doubted that; and she was marrying another man.

Sophie, as if following her thought, said suddenly: "Now, Dorcas, don't worry about Ronald. A broken heart won't kill him—men have died and worms have eaten them——"

"Don't . . ."

"My dear, I'm sorry. I didn't realize you felt so deeply about it—still. How long has it been since you saw him?"

"A month. I'll never see him again of course. I mean, not the same way. I suppose I'll see him somewhere now and then."

Sophie pondered and sighed. "Poor Ronald. After all, young men will be young men. I thought myself people were a little hard on him. Since he's known you, certainly he's done nothing out of the way."

Funny how grateful she felt to Sophie.

"It's done now," she said, her voice a little husky and uncertain. "It's too late——"

Sophie rose abruptly and stood there looking thoughtfully down at Dorcas. "It soon will be too late," she said and turned toward the door. With her hand on the doorknob she paused to look back at Dorcas. "I'll finish your packing after dinner.

You'd better rest now. Thank heaven there's nothing more for you to do but show up at the wedding tomorrow at twelve. Try to sleep. And forget about Ronald. Only listen, my dear; I never advise, you know that, but I'm going to now. Don't tell yourself you don't dare to see Ronald; that is admitting——"

She stopped, looking at Dorcas thoughtfully and a little remotely with her dark hazel eyes shadowed as if she were seeing someone else.

There was another small, heavy silence. Rain dashed gustily against the window beside her.

"Admitting what?"

Sophie's look became focused again upon Dorcas.

"Nothing," she said and went out and closed the door firmly behind her.

The room was very still after she'd gone. Still and growing darker, with only the two lights on the dressing table making little circles of cheer. Outside the rain whirled against the blackening windowpanes. Dorcas pulled an afghan over her feet and pushed the cushions so they were comfortable under her head and an hour later was still staring wide eyed at the high ceiling. Tomorrow at this time the wedding would be over. She would be on the train. Married. Going away on a honeymoon.

If only, now it was too late, she could forget the despairing look in Ronald's face when she had told him she was to marry Jevan! The things he had said—desperate things, threatening to kill himself; telling her he would always love her, throwing himself upon her mercy; and she'd had no mercy.

No one came into the room; Sophie had told them she was resting. She pushed away the cushions and afghan and got up, prowled to the window and back again. Lighted and put down a cigarette. Went back to the window and stared down at the cold, foggy night with the street lights making blobs of radiance and the pavements catching gleams of light from occasional passing cars.

The whole house was silent. They would bring her dinner on a tray.

She passed the table and there was the telephone and she stopped, oddly tempted. She knew Ronald's number. By taking up the telephone and murmuring a number she would hear his voice, talk to him, summon him from the confused oblivion to which her own act had cast him.

She locked both hands behind her.

What had Sophie told her to do? Oh yes, sort out the last minute odds and ends she intended to take with her.

She did so slowly. A sweater coat that would go in the trunk. Cold creams and bath sponges and powder to go in her dressing case. A little heap of things which Sophie might make use of—a tweed suit, a white velvet evening gown, two afternoon dresses; she folded them neatly and put them on a chair near the dressing table.

What else now? She glanced around the room and went to the boxes which had that afternoon arrived, and opened them. Stacks of underclothing, handmade with tiny, delicate stitches. She must pack them. Her trousseau.

She stood looking at them and after a moment thrust the lids back on the boxes again and turned away.

She paused at the dressing table; sat down and leaned forward to look at herself in the mirror. There might have been times when she could have thanked the Lord for a straight nose and fine skin and lovely, deep eye sockets. For deep blue eyes and a gay smile. For a soft masking of the firm Whipple chin. For glancing, evanescent moments of spiritual beauty. But it was not one of those times. She was pale and tired and lifeless looking. Beautiful bride indeed! She reached for powder puff and rouge; took up a new stick of lip paste and spread it heavily on her mouth. It was too deep a crimson, she thought, scrutinizing the face that now looked back at her from the mirror. She reached for blue eye shadow. And the telephone rang. Her own phone, there on the table. That meant the call was for her.

Who? Jevan or one of her bridesmaids.

But for a moment she did not move. And when she did get to the telephone and took it in her hand that hand was trembling. She said unsteadily: "Hello . . ."

It was Ronald. She had known it would be.

"Dorcas," he said. "Dorcas. Oh, my darling, I must see you. I've got to see you. Now."

CHAPTER 2

THE GLITTERING black windowpane reflected her eerily. Painted mouth and wide dark eyes; short rumpled brown hair; a green flannel housecoat wrapped tight around her. A telephone clutched to her breast.

She said almost in a whisper: "Ronald . . ."

"Darling, I've got to see you. I must see you. I can't bear it. Just one more time, Dorcas." Words poured feverishly into her ear. "Listen, dear; I've got it all planned. No one need know. I'll be at the corner of the house with a taxi at eight. Meet me there, darling. I'll bring you back any time you say. I won't—I won't beg or plead or—I won't do anything, my darling, but look at you. I've got to see you. Don't you understand, Dorcas? Just once more. Before you belong to another man."

It was like Ronald. Boyish. Impulsive. With anguish in his voice. But she couldn't meet him; it was impossible.

"You must come, Dorcas. I'll be there. I'll never ask another thing of you. Never. But I must see you."

"No. No."

"Why?"

"I——"

"Why not, Dorcas?"

She didn't answer and his voice acquired a sudden eagerness. "Are you afraid to meet me, Dorcas?"

Afraid? That was admitting—admitting what? she had asked Sophie, and Sophie had looked at her slowly and said: "Nothing."

"No, I'm not afraid. But I can't——"

"You can. You must. I'll be there, darling. At eight. Oh, Dorcas, it's so little I'm asking; only a crumb. To last me for the rest of my life."

The telephone clicked and was silent and he was gone.

She put it down slowly. She was excited, filled with a confused sense of exultation, dismay, guilt. And mainly of acute perplexity. She had, she knew now, longed for him to telephone, longed for him to make one last effort to see her. Now that he had done so she realized that to meet him would be the very height of folly.

She had seen him only once since her engagement was announced, so it was strange that her feeling toward him had so changed as her wedding drew near. But it had changed, for lately he haunted her thoughts, walked in her dreams, smiled at her, pleaded with her. Loved her.

But she couldn't meet him.

She found herself again at the window, shading her face with her hands and peering down at the street. He would be at that corner at eight; waiting in the shadow of the great oak trees in the rain. How long would he wait? An hour, perhaps, and turning hopefully at every sound.

She went back to the chaise longue and was sitting there, huddled tightly in her flannel coat, staring at the carpet when Sophie came in with a tray.

"I brought your dinner, honey," she said. "I'll finish packing while you eat. Then you can have a hot bath and go straight to bed and no one will bother you till morning."

She set the tray on a table and pulled it close to Dorcas and took the cover off a soup dish.

"Now then, eat your dinner," said Sophie briskly. "And tell me what to put in your bags."

Later Dorcas remembered that hour of indecision. Thinking of Ronald's words, of his voice; replying to Sophie's questions. "I must see you . . . darling . . . a crumb. To last me the rest of my life."

"Powder, Dorcas? This box? Rouge?"

"That's right. No, not that lipstick, it doesn't suit me. The blue eye shadow." Her own voice replying while Ronald repeated almost as if he were there: "Are you afraid—are you afraid—are you afraid——"

And all the time she was eating her dinner and listening for the gusts of rain against the glittering black windows. Once Sophie paused and went to the window and put her hand on the rope to pull the curtains and Dorcas stopped her sharply. "No, don't. I—I like the sound of the rain."

Sophie paused, gave her a surprised look, shrugged and went back to packing. Dorcas nervously touched her lips with her napkin; Ronald when he came would see the light from her windows. Ronald . . .

"Never mind packing the green suit," she said. "I'll leave some things here for you, Sophie, if you can make anything of them."

"Of course." Sophie glanced at the green tweed suit. "I can do with that suit, Dorcas. Thanks. . . . Well, that's about all."

The little clock on the dressing table said twenty minutes to eight when Sophie at last closed and locked the trunk. Dorcas' eyes were drawn to the clock again and again as if it were a magnet, and she was possessed by consuming impatience for Sophie to finish and leave. She wasn't going to meet Ronald; no. But it was important for her to be alone.

At ten minutes to eight Sophie at last took the tray and went away.

"I'll see to Cary," she said. "She's in bed already; had dinner on a tray and has a full supply of new magazines and a sleeping powder. Anything you want?"

"Nothing," said Dorcas, watching the clock.

"Oh. . . . Well, good night, my dear."

The door closed. Dorcas jumped to her feet.

Her hands flew; a comb through her short hair, which brought back the wave. Street shoes, brown oxfords with her own cold fingers trembling a little as she tied the laces. She took off her flannel coat; afterward she thought that if Sophie hadn't left the suit in the room she wouldn't have gone. But it was there, temptingly near at hand.

It took only a moment or two to pull on sweater and skirt and long, warm tweed jacket. Somewhere was a green hat for it; she found it and put it on. She did pause then to look at herself in the mirror and she knew in that moment that the thing she proposed to do was all wrong. It was not only foolishly weak, childishly and falsely romantic but it was dishonest. She would be in a few hours time the wife of another man and she owed him, at least, loyalty.

And quite deliberately, with a frightened determination, she stifled that small voice with a specious argument.

It was the last night of her own. The last night she was to be Dorcas Whipple, responsible only to herself. After the wedding ceremony she would be a good and faithful wife. But never again for all the rest of her life would she be entirely free and entirely herself. Therefore why should she not see Ronald?

It was specious and she knew it. She fumbled at the fasten-

ing of the red fox collar that rose high around her face and
might have taken off the coat. In that instant not only her own
destiny but that of at least three other people hung in balance.

And she caught a glimpse in the mirror of her bare left
hand. Tomorrow there would be a wedding ring there; a
band that would bind her tightly from then on to her own
ideas of decency and honesty. After tomorrow Dorcas Whipple would be Dorcas Locke—a different woman.

It was like losing her own identity. And Ronald, a part of
that old, familiar life, was waiting in the rain and darkness.
Waiting only to say good-by to her.

She turned swiftly from the mirror and out of the room.
She went quietly so no one would hear and question. There
was no one in the hall and a light burned beyond the old-
fashioned transom above her mother's bedroom door.

She went down the stairs and still there was no one. The
servants probably were busy in the back of the house. Her
own latchkey was in a little drawer of the Jacobean chest
near the door. She took it and let herself out and walked rapidly down the shrublined sidewalk and out the tall iron gate.

Her real distress was shot with a trivial embarrassment;
she was stealing out to a clandestine meeting on the very eve
of her wedding. She ought to have felt ashamed but actually
she felt only rather silly and childish. As if she were acting
in some play and doing it badly.

Why hadn't Ronald simply come to the house and demanded to see her? But he couldn't of course. Cary would
have known and stopped it.

Her heart gave a leap into her throat, however, as she saw
him—a shadowy, slender figure in an overcoat with his hat
pulled down over his face. He heard her footsteps and ran
lightly to meet her.

"My darling," he cried, "I knew you'd come," and took
her hands and held them to his lips.

A car passed them rather slowly, its tires swishing. Dorcas
was only vaguely aware of it.

His face was hot, his lips shaking a little. Without intending to she pulled her hands away abruptly.

"I only came to say good-by," she said lamely. "I——"

"One little hour," said Ronald. "That's all I ask. All I
shall ever ask. The taxi's waiting around the corner. You
can't stand here in the rain——"

"I can't stay. I must go back now. I only came——"

"You came," said Ronald in an exultant, breathless whisper. "That's enough."

They were at the corner and a taxi was there, its lights dimmed so they made wan streaks along the wet pavements. A dash of rain struck her face sharply as they crossed to the curb, then they were in the taxi.

"But, Ronald——"

"Hush, dear." He leaned forward. "Thirty-six Schumanze Court. And hurry."

The taxi jumped ahead.

"No, no, Ronald. Tell him to stop. I must not stay——"

"Hush, darling. You don't want him to hear everything we have to say each other."

"But——"

"Don't be silly, sweet. I'm not going to abduct you. But I must talk to you a little alone. Don't deny me that small thing, Dorcas. I've gone through such hell. We'll go up to my apartment; there's no one there and we can talk a little. I'll take you back at nine. I swear it, Dorcas. That's one hour for me to remember for the rest of my life. One little hour——"

"This is all wrong, Ronald. Useless."

"An hour of farewell," he said. "Farewell to yourself, Dorcas. After tomorrow——"

If he had touched her, if he had taken her hands again, if he had seemed in any way unresigned, she would still have gone back.

But he did not.

Later she wondered about it.

It was perhaps a fifteen-minute ride. Later, too, she remembered the dusk in the taxi, the swish of tires, the sense of waves along the breakwater and of fog-haloed lights when they turned onto Michigan and crossed the bridge. He said almost nothing and once she felt actually and for a fleeting moment as if the man seated there beside her in the dusk were a stranger. He seemed in the flesh and in the twilight of the taxi different, indescribably changed from the man who during the past few weeks had been so constantly in her mind. Well, now she could tell him she had been unjust; tell him how deeply she regretted any pain she had caused him, wipe the slate clean of any bitterness between them. Yes, she could do that and they would remember each other pleasantly and with friendliness. Without pain.

She sat in the dusk, planning.

Ronald's apartment was in a roomy, oldish building just off the Drive and around the corner of Schumanze Court; she had been there before to cocktail parties and to occasional small dinner parties of eight or ten, served by a caterer, for his only servant was a Japanese who came in by the day. There was a smallish and rather shabby hall, an elevator and a narrow flight of stairs. The rent was probably exorbitant. The building did boast, too, a doorman, who ran to open the door of the taxi as they stopped and then, obviously torn, left them abruptly to hurry toward another car which drove up slowly behind them.

The little elevator was in use and they walked up the stairs to the second floor. Ronald's apartment was on the corner, overlooking during clear days a small slice of blue lake, a garage immediately below, and above and against the sky heaped cliffs of apartment buildings. The corridor itself was rather narrow, stretching away past a transverse corridor on which the elevator opened, to a dim red light at the far end indicating a fire escape. Ronald took out keys. The door was painted white and had a plain, old-fashioned lock—the kind which is not, when you close the door, self-locking.

"Do you always remember to lock the door from the inside?" said Dorcas idly, watching him insert the key, and was to remember it later.

"No," said Ronald and smiled a little bitterly. "But I have so little to steal. Come in, my dear." He closed the door behind them. "I promise to watch the clock. Let me take your coat. It's always hot in here."

She looked at him a little shyly in the white glow of the modernistic lamps. She had been wrong; he was exactly the same—clear, incredibly handsome profile, bright eyes, wavy blond hair, small, delicately curved mouth. "A weak mouth," Cary had said. "One look at that mouth ought to convince you, Dorcas."

Her mother's words floated into her memory as she turned and let him take her tweed coat. She pushed the memory away; besides, it didn't matter and was not important, for after tonight she would never see Ronald Drew again.

He took the coat and put it down on a white divan. His

own followed it. He hesitated, reached for a white cigarette box with tiny mirrors set in it, then put down the box and came back to Dorcas.

His eyes were very bright.

"I lied to you," he said. "I lied to you to get you here. Now I'm never going to let you go."

Before she could move or even sense what he said he took her tightly, almost feverishly in his arms.

CHAPTER 3

SHE WASN'T frightened. Even as he bent her head back, kissing her, she wasn't at all frightened, for the curious sensation of playing a role in some vague, unrehearsed play returned to her. She felt, however, very uncomfortable and very much ashamed. After all, said a small, cold voice inside her even as she pulled abruptly away from him, after all, she had invited it.

But she didn't like it.

"Don't," she cried violently and heard her own strangled voice with a kind of surprise at its agitation. "*Don't!*"

She was fairly strong herself; slender muscles hardened by swimming and tennis. She wriggled away from him and stood there facing him, trying to steady her breath while he watched her. There were two scarlet patches in his cheeks; his eyes were still bright and had something in them she had never seen there before.

"You needn't scream," he said rather sulkily and unsteadily. "I won't eat you."

Had she screamed?

"That was silly. I'm going now."

For an instant she had the fantastic notion that he was going to put her out himself—angrily, throwing her coat after her. It was fantastic; it flickered across her mind as irrationally as a hot little wind might have done. For immediately he was all apology.

"No, don't go, Dorcas. I'm sorry. I'm terribly sorry. It's just that I—I love you so," he said pleadingly. "I won't do it

again. I promise. But we can't part like this. Can we, darl—
Dorcas. Wait. Sit here on the divan. I'll go across the room."

Again he didn't touch her or attempt to lead her to a chair.
Instead he pleaded with her, abjectly, throwing himself again
on her mercy.

"I love you so, Dorcas. I love you so and it's the last time
I shall see you. You promised me——"

"You promised *me*," said Dorcas and went to the divan
and took her coat in her hands.

In the mirror above the deep divan she caught a glimpse
of his face and the sheer, stark dismay that flashed upon it.
A dismay so lost, so terrified that it was as if a drowning man
had missed in his last desperate clutch for a rope. It was poignant, it was sharply real; it was nothing short of despair. The
uneasy feeling of playing a part in a futile and slightly taw-
dry theatrical performance dropped suddenly away from
her. She turned in honest contrition.

"I'm sorry, Ronald. I'm desperately sorry things have
happened—just this way. I—I shall always value your friend-
ship and—and remember . . ." She meant exactly what she
said but she found the words difficult, for he looked as if he
did not understand her and as if he were thinking of something else.

"Dear Dorcas," he said flatly and added abruptly: "I need
a drink. Wait a second, Dorcas. I—I won't bother you again.
Honest. We'll have a drink and a smoke and I'll take you
back home. One last little talk together for the sake of—of
all our good times."

It was exactly as if he had reverted to the lines of the
play; as if she groped for her cues but he knew them all,
so again the feeling of unreality, of cheap theatricalism swept
over her. Yet what he said had exactly the right tone of
friendliness, and she had seen that look of bitterness and pain
in his face and that was real.

He turned rapidly and went out before she could reply.
She sat down rather limply in the deep white divan. She was
at the same time confused and angry; contrite and pitying.
Well, she would go at once.

She could hear him moving about in the small kitchen
down a narrow passage. Mirrors everywhere observed her
from dull blue walls. White furniture; white rugs with black
stripes, great soft white cushions. Mirrors in tables; tables in
mirrors. Accustomed to the comfortable Victorian clutter of

the Whipple house, the room seemed to Dorcas vaguely unpleasant, the blue walls pasty, the whites dead and somber,
the spaces too empty. Her plain green tweeds were curiously
out of place.

As she was out of place. Well, Ronald would be back immediately. They would have a moment or two of amicable
understanding and she would go home. Odd how depressing
all that white was. It was so quiet that the sudden sound of
a car in the garage below, starting with a series of backfires,
seemed near and loud.

Other times when she had been in the apartment there had
been gayety, voices, glitter. Now there was nothing of that.

Queer how the mirrors watched her.

It was a small apartment. There was a fairly large living
room, a bedroom and bath, a narrow hall running parallel
to the bedroom wall back to a small kitchen, where just then,
unexpectedly, there was a sound, repeated, as if a door had
opened and closed.

Without any reason at all it startled her and she listened.
It was not repeated but certainly there was another sound—
whispering? No. The sound became more distinct and it
was only ice being chipped and dropped into glasses. It must
have been the refrigerator door that opened and closed. She
sat back again.

And knew she must go. Then. That very instant. It was
the strangest and strongest compulsion, as if someone had
spoken to her—urgently and with knowledge.

Her coat was beside her; it was only a few steps to the
door. Departure now would bring things to an end and
would spare her any danger of a further scene with Ronald.
But she did want desperately to part with him honestly and
with friendliness.

So she hesitated and Ronald returned. He had a tray and
glasses filled with ice, a three-cornered bottle and a seltzer
bottle.   ·

He put the tray on the low table before the divan and
filled the glasses.

"One highball," he said, smiling at her over the seltzer bottle. "One cigarette, then I'll take you home. Here's to you,
Dorcas. And I—I only want you to be happy."

She took the glass he put in her hand. He lifted his own,
looked brightly at her over the rim and drank thirstily.

"Drink it, Dorcas." He poured himself another glass, went

to the door leading to the passage and closed it and returned to look down at her.

"I forgot how you hate whisky," he said. "But honest, Dorcas, there's not another thing to drink in the place. Drinking doesn't happen to be one of my failings." He said the last bitterly and added: "They were all against me, weren't they, Dorcas? Oh, you needn't answer. I know. Everybody you knew in all Chicago came to your mother and warned her against me. Rightly perhaps, Dorcas. Except—except I loved you. I still love you. I shall always love you. You can't stop it——"

"Ronald, don't. It—it doesn't help——"

"Oh yes, it helps. I'm having the satisfaction of telling you that. I'll never have it again. Unless—are you going to let me see you after you are married? No! No, of course not. I didn't think so. You needn't look like that, as if I'd offended you. You——"

"Ronald, I'm going now." He was talking oddly, jerkily, as if he'd already been drinking a great deal. She rose and again that look of something closely akin to despair flashed across his flushed, handsome face.

"Wait, Dorcas," he said hurriedly, putting down his glass and reaching for cigarettes. "One last cigarette. Then we'll go. I promised." He came to her with the small, mirrored box extended. "Drink the highball, honey. It'll warm you up before you go out into this fiendish night. . . . I'll light your cigarette for you."

There was a small electric lighter. His hand holding the little torch was altogether steady in spite of his feverish manner.

She put the cigarette to her lips and accepted the light. The one swallow of whisky and soda had stung her throat and the puff of smoke was bitter and unpleasant. Aware of his sudden silence, she looked up; he was standing above her, his hand still holding the little torch, his eyes very bright and focused oddly, not at her but as if there were something beyond her, over her shoulder, across the room. And as if that something moved a little, for his eyes moved—fixedly and brightly as a cat's eyes, stalking.

It was a fantastic impression but so strong that she put down her glass and turned. There was, of course, nobody. Unless—unless the blank white door leading to the kitchen passage had just closed.

"What is it, Dorcas? What's wrong?"

"That—door—moved." She was still staring at it. Had it moved? But it couldn't have.

"Oh, nonsense!"

"Yes, I saw it, Ronald. I'm sure—or at least I thought——"

"Do you mean to say you saw it move?"

"N-no. Not exactly. But——"

"Oh, come, Dorcas! Don't be a dear little silly. How could the door move? It's fast shut and there's no one but you and me in the whole apartment. No one."

She looked perplexedly at the wide, blank white panels. Certainly the door did not move now; certainly that split second during which she saw—or thought she saw—the door barely tremble into place had been an illusion. All those mirrors about the room were deceiving as to perspective and motion. She could see herself and Ronald standing above her at a dozen different angles and views.

And she was to go. Now.

She half rose and reached for her coat and Ronald put his hand on her shoulder lightly but held her in her seat.

"Ronald——"

"Yes, dear little Dorcas. When you've finished your cigarette. I'm giving you up for a lifetime, my darling, but not until"—he glanced at the small clock on a table across the room, a blue-faced clock with stars on it and white hands, tipped in stars—"not until nine o'clock. At least ten minutes more. It will take you that long to finish your cigarette. And your whisky."

The hand on her shoulder, curiously, annoyed her. She moved away from him to the other end of the divan and as she did so he sat down beside her.

"Listen, Dorcas," he began. "There are some things I want to say to you. Don't get upset but please listen to me." He paused, turning his glass in his fingers, watching it with absent, bright eyes. "In the first place you don't love Jevan."

"I——"

"Don't talk yet, I want to finish. You don't love him. I love you and you—you love me, my dear. I know you do. I know in a hundred ways. I—well, this is the point: now that it has come right down to marrying him you don't want to. I know that too. That's one of the reasons I waited until now. So long as the marriage was far enough in the future you yielded to your mother. I'm not blaming you, my darling, for listening to what they told you of me. Too much of it, perhaps, was true. *Was* true, Dorcas—*is* true no longer, since I met you."

He paused again. Dorcas made a motion to speak and stopped. He was talking calmly and with a kind of reasonableness and everything he said, Dorcas told herself, was true. Yet mainly she was aware of an increasing uneasiness. Of the mirrors. Of the white, blank door behind her.

"But now that your marriage is so near you, you realize the truth, Dorcas. Well then . . ." He put down the glass, turned to her and took her hands. "Why go on with it?"

"The wedding——"

"The wedding! Don't go through with it. People will wonder and exclaim but will forget."

"But—but I—my mother——"

"She has lived her life. She can't live your life."

"Jevan——"

"Listen to me. Does he love you?"

She hesitated, held by the glowing brightness of his eyes, thinking confusedly of Jevan, of the man beside her, of her own uncertainties, of the door behind her which had not moved.

"Does he love you? Do you love him, Dorcas?" Again leaning close to her, holding her hands tightly, he waited, furiously intent. And again answered for her: "No. For you love me, Dorcas. And you must marry me. Now. Tomorrow."

His face was flushed; his bright eyes shining; his hands feverish in their grip. And something was wrong about the still, watchful room.

"No. No, I can't."

"Why not? You love me; why marry him? It's impossible, Dorcas. You must come with me."

No time to think this thing out. No time to analyze. No time to do anything but pull your hands away and shrink back into the corner of the divan and look swiftly around the room. No one was there of course. No one but Ronald and herself.

"No, no, Ronald."

"Why?"

Why?

"Because—oh, I can't, Ronald. I simply can't. You must not ask me——"

His face was a dark, angry crimson.

"Don't just repeat that over and over again, Dorcas. Of course you can. Who's going to stop you? Who can stop you?"

"I—I can't. It's too late. Everything's ready. I can't—I'm going now. I must go." She tried to rise. And he caught her suddenly again in his arms, suddenly and closely so she could not move, and the reasonableness in his voice departed. He cried:

"You are not! You are going to stay here! We'll elope tonight if you like. I don't care when. Or where. We can drive to Waukegan or Crown Point and be married tonight. But you're going to marry me, Dorcas. You don't love him. You love me. You—you wouldn't have come here with me if you hadn't loved me. Not the night before your wedding."

"No—no, Ronald! Let me go!" The sudden, sharp violence of compulsion in her voice seemed to reach him, for he said more quietly: "Very well." His arms dropped and she was on her feet and he looked at her and said: "I'll kill myself, Dorcas, rather than lose you."

He said it unexpectedly, looking up at her with those bright secret eyes. It ought to have moved her. It did move her but inexplicably not to compassion; instead to sudden mysterious rage.

"It's all very neat," she cried in sharp fury. "Young man's apartment; liquor and love-making; suicide threats; Waukegan or Crown Point or else. Oh, Ronald, how—how childish of you to stage such a trite little scene!"

He lay back against the divan staring fixedly up at her. His handsome face was still a little flushed; he was smiling rather gently but there was again in his bright eyes a queer, unfathomable look of calculation.

Dorcas was too angry—angry with herself, angry with Ronald—to notice that look. She went around the low table and snatched her coat. There wasn't any room for composure or dignity or poise; she was thoroughly in a rage and hated herself more than she hated Ronald. She took her coat with the gesture of a shrew and cried sharply: "You've spoiled everything. I came here because I"—(Because she loved him? Because all during that month of absence she had grown more and more convinced that she loved him?)—"because I wanted to see you again. Because I wanted us to remember each other kindly and as friends. You've spoiled everything. You've made it cheap and false. I'll never remember you again with anything but loathing. I thought it was real—the way you felt. I thought you——"

"Stop that. Don't be a fool, Dorcas. Or a silly, stupid child. After all, tomorrow you're to be married; you ought not to be so disturbed by a little love-making tonight. Besides, it's me you're going to marry."

She jerked on her coat. She wouldn't reply, wouldn't listen. He lay back against the deep divan, watching her with a curious lassitude and assurance. Apparently he was going to let her go without further words. Well, that was good. She turned toward the door without speaking—caught a glimpse of her own disheveled hair in a mirror above a white face and blazing eyes and a mouth heavily painted with new and unfamiliar lipstick. Where was her hat?

She whirled back. It lay on the divan where it had fallen during that absurd struggle with Ronald. Again, sharply and with fury in her gesture, she snatched the hat. And again reached the door without a backward glance when Ronald laughed.

It was a singular kind of laugh, slow and easy and assured, but it had no mirth in it.

Something chill and a little frightened stirred suddenly below her rage. She turned to look at him again and he said, smiling:

"You can't leave, darling. I've been a thorough, complete scoundrel and locked the door. I'm not going to open it until—to quote again from the fine old melodramas from which I have lavishly borrowed—until you are mine."

Scorn and rage and that chill thing stirring below.

"Ronald, don't be such a complete idiot. Open the door."

"No, my sweet."

"Ronald, you can't possibly be serious. This is preposterous."

"Yes, isn't it. I tried to think of some other way. Really I did, darling. But after all, it does work now and then, you know. Or might when women are worth the trouble. As you are, darling. As you——" He was rising slowly from the divan. Certainly he was going to open the door. Certainly it was a poor idea of a joke. Suppose—suppose it wasn't? With the sharp irrelevance of a nightmare she thought of the bridesmaids arriving in yellow chiffons at St Chrystofer's and the bride shut up in an apartment with a man who'd taken leaves of his senses.

Ronald came nearer. "As you are worth it, sweet," he said and reached behind her. Incredibly he touched the electric light switch and the chill stirring thing away back in her mind leaped to terror as he found her in the tumultuous, frantic darkness.

A telephone was ringing. She knew that.

It rang again and again, somewhere away from that hot, panting area of struggle, somewhere off in the thick darkness. She knew when he suddenly left her, so suddenly and savagely relinquishing her that she almost fell. She heard him groping in the darkness; then he found a table lamp and turned on the light. She had one glimpse of his face above the light—foreshortened as he bent downward—the face of a man she had never seen, with mirrors all around and a blank white door behind him.

The telephone pealed demandingly. He found it at last on a table and thrust it over savagely so it fell on the floor and was disconnected.

Dorcas reached the door and it was not locked at all. She pulled the door open and all her life afterward remembered the sound of it as it closed, shutting off Ronald's voice.

Ten minutes later, on Lake Shore Drive, she hailed a cruising taxi and gave the driver her address. It seemed to her that he looked at her curiously. But why not? A girl wandering around alone in the street in weather like that. Or was it because he noted something of the agitation she felt?

She huddled back in a corner of the seat. It must have turned much colder, for she was trembling all over. She had to lock her teeth together. She tried to count and draw long breaths; one, two, three, inhale—one, two, three, exhale.

She was still counting when they reached the Whipple house, which loomed high and dark into the squally, gusty night.

CHAPTER 4

LUCKILY there was money in her pocket; barely enough for the driver and a small tip. As she turned from the taxi some oddly repetitive experience caught at her; a car was just turning the corner ahead of the taxi and it was going slowly, as if it were in second gear. As if, then, it had been either idling or stopped at the Whipple drive. But no one would be calling just then. Then she knew why it had seemed a familiar and repeated experience: twice before that night she had been aware of a car driving slowly along the street. That was all.

She went into the house, grateful for the solidity of the door and the indescribably familiar fragrances of the old house.

No one was in the hall, though lights were burning, and she saw no one on the stairs.

No one in the upper hall either, though as she opened her own door some instinct compelled her to turn quickly to look again down the hall. It was, however, dimly lighted and stretched away into quiet, apparently empty shadows, and if it had been a sound that caught her attention it was not repeated. Her room was like a haven and it was blessedly warm, yet long after she had gone to bed she was still cold and shaken and confused. But she was mainly terribly tired, too tired to think, too tired to analyze. Too tired even to exorcise a queer, cold horror.

She left the bedside light burning. She had turned it off once but the moment darkness enfolded her she was back at the door of Ronald's apartment with the mirrors watching her and the blank white door seeming about to close itself. She put a desperate little hand into the darkness and turned on the light again, sighing shakily as her own familiar room came mellowly into view and she lay there keeping her eyes fastened on the tall mahogany bedpost until from desperate weariness she went to sleep. Once during the night, however, she must have dreamed, for she was conscious suddenly, strugglingly, of the white door. Only now and to her half-awakened consciousness it had something horrible and terrifying about it and instead of closing it was about to open.

She turned, twisted, escaped the dream, if dream it was and not awakening, and went to sleep again.

Morning dawned cold and gray with a vicious wind off the lake.

There was an early bustle in the Whipple house, though Dorcas heard none of it. Among the several servants there was none who remembered any other Whipple wedding and only one or two who had been in the Whipple house for more than a few years, but still the event was of sufficient and distracting importance. But Sophie had given orders and the bustle did not extend itself to the front part of the second floor. So while the front steps were being scrubbed and the two cars given a glistening rub in the big garage, while flowers and boxes from the caterers arrived in a steady and increasingly heavy stream at the back door and telegrams and last-minute packages at the front door, there was still only the faintest echo of all that activity in the big, silent rooms on the second floor where Cary and Dorcas slept. Sophie was up at six, neat and smart and trim in a brown knitted dress, superintending.

But not a sound of it all crept into Cary's room, with its heat and its heavy curtains, its thick carpets, its cushioned chairs. It was a huge room, heavier, even, in appearance than Dorcas' room, for Cary had shared it with Pennyforth Whipple—it and the gloomy dressing room lined with mirrors and cupboards and the enormous bathroom with a tub so big that Cary always, in all those years, felt lost and a little afraid in its depths. Penn Whipple had had ideas of furniture; first it should be big, for he was a big man; second it should be comfortable, for he liked comfort; third, regrettably, it should be enduring.

So it was all three and at night when Cary was sleepless the great dark shapes standing about the walls seemed to move noiselessly as if they possessed a secret, sluggish life of their own.

Dorcas' room had been relieved a little of the oppressive effect of so much heavy mahogany by chintzes here and there; by wallpaper with a pleasant little design and a gayly flounced dressing table; by a frivolously pillowed chaise longue and many low, open bookshelves. She woke about nine and lay there for a moment looking at the familiar little gilt french clock on the bookshelf nearest her.

Almost nine and there was a compulsion about getting up on that particular morning; she sat up in bed and reached for slippers before she was wide enough awake to know what that compulsion was.

Her wedding.

At noon. And it was already nine.

The room was cold with a chill, dreary wind blowing in at the windows. She ran across, shivering in her thin pajamas, and closed the windows and automatically unfastened and let fall the green curtains which Mamie, every night when she turned down the beds, looped up away from the windows to protect them from the soot in the night air. It was a dark morning; the little bedside lamp, still burning, made a small area of cheer until she remembered why she had left it burning.

The memory of Ronald and of the distorted little scene in his apartment gave her a moment of shock.

It was a queer kind of shock, obscurely warning, as if, unexpectedly and entirely without warning, an earthquake had given a faint, premonitory little shake, stirring itself.

For there was actually something premonitory about that memory. She looked at the clock again and put her finger on the bell. There were many things to do: breakfast, last-minute notes she herself must write, dressing; probably Jevan would either come to the house or telephone.

But even then her marriage to Jevan seemed far in the future—at least Jevan seemed far in the future. In three hours she was to be married to a man she did not love, yet her common sense, her feeling for the fitness of things, induced in her a kind of detached acceptance of it. The sense of panic of the previous night had gone and she thrust aside the nightmarish experience with Ronald. It was morning, she was herself again; she was that day to make a good and suitable marriage and the man she was marrying she had known so long (and, she thought, so well) that he was at once familiar and remote.

She thought once, however, with something sharp and acute in that thought which would not have been there on the previous day, that there was nothing at all emotional in her relationship with Jevan or in what that relationship would be after marriage. It was a subtly soothing, reassuring thought. In those weeks of what she supposed must be a kind of sensible, conventional devotion, there had been on Jevan's part no strenuous love-making. His kiss on her cheek was cool and brief; he was pleasant, friendly, attentive in all the gestures but remote. It lulled her that morning, the grateful thought of that cool, unemotional friendliness. She did wonder once, lying back in the fragrant warmth of the huge square tub, if she had been too preoccupied during those weeks with other things, with—say it, Dorcas; admit it—with Ronald; if she had thought too little of the fact that she was marrying Jevan Locke—binding their two lives together for always.

She thrust that thought away too. There would be time to think later—or she ought to have done it before now. Certainly the very morning of her wedding was no time to engage upon such futile speculations as those were. The thing to do now was have breakfast, be ready for Mamie to dress her hair, see her mother.

Cary herself came in when Mamie, the elderly maid, brought in Dorcas' breakfast tray.

Cary was pale and nervous; her small, slender body was wrapped in a thin pink negligee and she looked cold but it was Cary's firm belief that any negligee must be diaphanous and that all blondes wore pink.

"Good morning, darling," she said nervously. "Did you sleep, Dorcas? Mamie, you'd better light the fire; it's terribly cold in here. I suppose you've had every window in the room wide open all night. How can you stand this horrible smoky, damp air? Risking getting penumonia on your wedding day! There, there, dear, I didn't mean to scold."

"All right, Mom. I know."

She kissed her mother's soft cheek, put her feet again into warm, sheepskin-lined slippers and went to the tray. There was the pleasant, homely odor of hot coffee and muffins.

Mamie, kneeling, lighted the old-fashioned gas log in the grate which, as always, sputtered and hissed. In a few moments it would be desperately hot in the room; fine blue points danced before Dorcas' eyes. Cary sat down in an easy chair before the fire.

"Coffee, Mom?"

"No. Thank you, dear. I've had breakfast—quite early. I couldn't sleep." She sighed. Mamie gave her a practiced look and went briefly away to return at once with a woolen shawl which she put about her mistress's slender shoulders.

"Thank you, Mamie." Cary huddled in the shawl. "Such a

wretched day, Dorie, for your wedding. I did so hope the
sun would shine."

"Never mind," said Dorcas consolingly. "The church will
look nice; yellow calla lilies and jonquils along the rail will
be bright. And the yellow bridesmaids' gowns will look
cheerful too. And the lights. Nobody will ever think about
it being a dark day. Yes, Mamie?"

"What time will you want to dress, Miss Dorcas?"

What time? Dorcas ignored the sudden little stab the question gave her. Too late to back out now; too late to start
worrying, too late to do anything but go ahead. Dress, go
to the church, stand there in white satin and make promises
she must keep.

"Ten," said Cary quickly, answering for her, and Dorcas
nodded. That gave her two hours to dress and get to the
church—too much time for dressing, but then, it was better
not to have too much time of her own.

Mamie went quietly away. Cary moved, sighed, touched
her carefully waved gray hair with unsteady, slender fingers and said: "Dorcas, is it all right? About your marriage,
I mean. I"—she hesitated, leaned forward and spoke in a
jerky little rush as if what she said had been pent up for a long
time—"I wouldn't want you to marry anyone you really
don't love, my dear. I've been afraid I urged you too much.
Afraid I had no right to—to interfere about Ronald. Tell me,
Dorcas——"

Ronald. Dorcas took a muffin and applied herself to butter
and marmalade and wouldn't look at her mother.

"It's all right, Mother. Don't worry, please. I know as well
as I could ever know anything that you only want me to be
happy and well cared for."

"Oh, Dorcas, are you sure?" There was an appeal in her
mother's soft voice that was touched with desperation. "Are
you sure Ronald means nothing to you now? If I could only
be certain of that."

Something inside Dorcas winced. She thought tersely that
she was certain about nothing.

There was a little silence and she tried not to see Ronald's
face as she had seen it in that last second with the white door
behind him about to open. . . . No, that was her dream. But
Ronald's face above the light was not a dream.

She must reply, for her mother was leaning forward, pale
with anxiety, dark circles under her eyes, her mouth tremu-

lous, her small thin hands clutched together. Dorcas forced herself to look straight into her mother's eyes.

"Listen, dear," she said steadily. "I was upset yesterday. Uneasy, nervous—as if something was going to go wrong. Some catastrophe—some——" A dark, quick fear leaped into her mother's eyes. Dorcas went on hurriedly: "But it was sheer nervous apprehension. This morning I'm—I'm myself again. Common sense—you know, Mom, you've always said I had that——"

"You are very like your father," murmured Cary automatically.

"Whatever it is, anyway, has come to my rescue. I have known Jevan for a long time, remember. There's no reason why it can't be a successful and reasonably happy marriage."

"That's not enough, Dorcas," said her mother suddenly. "I was wrong—oh, I was wrong, my dear! If you loved Ronald——"

Dorcas got up and walked quickly to the window so her mother could not see her face. She said over her shoulder, a little crisply, trying to cover any betraying emotion in her voice: "I do not love Ronald."

There was a long silence. Outside the bare trees bent under the wind; the gray sky hung almost as low as the housetops, holding dark swirls of smoke close and heavy. The pavement below was black and wet. In another hour or two she would be crossing that pavement, holding up her satin train with something put down to keep her silver slippers dry. Entering the car, riding with her mother and Sophie and Marcus Pett to the church.

Cary, behind her, was crying tremulously, in little gasps. Dorcas turned but her mother put up her hands as if to ward her off.

"Never mind, darling," she said shakily. "Don't bother—I —it's only that I'm terribly glad."

"Glad——"

"Glad you don't love Ronald. You were telling me the truth, weren't you, Dorcas? You were telling me the truth? I lay awake all night——"

Dorcas knelt beside her mother and took her frail little figure in her arms. She felt strong and young and competent.

"There now, Mom dear. I mean it. Understand? You can count on that, and I'll do my very best to make my marriage

—happy," finished Dorcas. "Happy" wasn't the word but it satisfied her mother.

"I'm sorry, Dorcas. I didn't mean to—to cry. But you're my baby."

"I know, dear."

"I want you to be happy. But you—you couldn't have been with Ronald."

Again something cold and ugly stirred in Dorcas. She remembered the sick revulsion she had felt at Ronald's touch. Well, Cary didn't know and mustn't know.

"There now, Mom. Pull yourself together, dear. Everything's all right and you have to get dressed, too, you know. I won't have my pretty mother sitting there in the pew with red eyes."

"No, of course; I'm so silly. I must look nice. You do like my gray chiffon, don't you, Dorcas?"

"I love it. And you in it. Pink your cheeks a little and——"

"Your father would have been so proud today. Proud and sorry to give you up. As I am, my daughter."

"You won't be giving me up. I won't give you up."

"No, that's right; you'll be gone only two months. Is everything packed?"

"Everything. Sophie will see the house is properly closed and you and she are to go straight off to Sulphur Springs for six weeks. Then when you get back I shall be here and you must help me furnish our new apartment. We've done nothing yet."

"It would be nice if you were going to live here," said Cary wistfully. "But then it's better to have your own place. Although it's a good thing Jevan is closing and selling the old Locke house: it has served its time. You will stay here until you find just the place you want, won't you, dear?"

"Yes, of course."

Cary, smiling mistily at her daughter, dabbed her eyes with her soft little hand.

"You've been a good daughter."

"Now, Mom—I mustn't cry too."

"No. Oh, dear no, you must look lovely. You are so pretty, dear. I know I've never seen a more beautiful bride. If only your father——"

"Mother, all this trust fund business—I mean, when it's turned over to me I'm going to try to help Jevan manage it."

A faint worried frown went over her mother's face. Business to Cary was mysterious and dreadful and terrifying and it was altogether something which only the broad shoulders of men were fitted to bear.

"Yes, yes, Dorcas," she said. "But Jevan is so capable. It will be better just to turn things over to him."

"Oh, I shall. I can't do anything else now. But eventually, when I know more about it——"

Sophie came into the room.

She didn't knock; there was no announcement of her coming. She simply opened the door and walked in and stood there, closing the door slowly behind her.

"Dorcas——"

Her face was as white as the newspaper she held. There were black headlines. She said: "Ronald Drew committed suicide last night. . . . Oh, good God, Cary, don't faint."

But she did. Neatly, immediately at Dorcas' feet, a little huddled heap of pink chiffon sliding slowly out of the chair.

"Mother!"

"Get the salts. Ring for Mamie! Get water——"

Sophie was kneeling, holding that ashen-faced, limp little heap in her arms. Someone—not Dorcas but someone who took charge of Dorcas' body—was running. Pressing the bell frantically, shouting for Mamie, bringing dripping wet towels.

That someone said in the voice of a sleepwalker: "Ronald . . ."

"He committed suicide last night with his own revolver. He was found early this morning. It's in all the papers—all over town. For God's sake, Dorcas, if you faint, too, I·don't know what I'll do! Open the window and lean out. Get yourself some brandy. Anything——"

Sophie leaned anxiously over Cary, holding the dripping towel to her soft throat.

"Anything," she cried sharply. "But don't go to pieces now. It's only two hours until the wedding."

That scene last night, then, had not been theatrical and cheap—it had been real. Dorcas had been blind, stupid, horrible in her selfish obtuseness.

She knelt down beside Sophie.

"I won't—I can't—go on with the wedding."

CHAPTER 5

As Mamie opened the door the telephone began to ring. It kept on ringing during most of that chaotic morning and Sophie finally took it off the hook and left it on the table, where now and then it still buzzed dully and insistently so it was a kind of demanding murmur, queerly imperative, under all those other voices. Just then, however, it was only Mamie's voice.

"Let me take her. Help me carry her, Miss Sophie. Take her feet, Miss Dorcas. Over there on the lounge. Now then. . . . Put her head lower. . . ." Mamie knew exactly what to do. Bench, the middle-aged houseman, came with brandy, his hands trembling as he poured it.

It was not a long faint. Cary sighed, sighed heavily again, opened her eyes and remembered, for she fastened those faded, lovely blue eyes on Dorcas and said weakly:

"Oh, my darling. On your wedding day."

The telephone rang again. Sophie, her lips set, went to answer it.

"Give Miss Dorcas brandy too," she said crisply to Bench and took the telephone. "Yes. . . . Yes, this is Sophie. Yes, we've heard. . . . Cary's all right now." Above the telephone she met Cary's anxious blue eyes. ("It's Marcus," said Sophie in parentheses.) "Yes, Marcus. Yes, everything's quite all right. We're going right on with the wedding. Yes, I agree. . . ." She looked at Cary again. "He says if we need him he'll come right away."

"*No!*" cried Dorcas. "Tell him I won't—I won't—there can't be a wedding after that."

Ronald . . . Ronald, as she had seen him last . . . Ronald . . .

Somebody put a glass of brandy in her hand. Her mother was sitting up now, her lips gray but color coming back to her face. She was all right then. Automatically, always, Cary was the first consideration.

"I think you'd better come, Marcus," Sophie was saying. "Yes, right away——"

"*No!*" cried Dorcas. "No. Nothing anybody can say——"

"Dorcas, the wedding! Everything's arranged. We can't possibly change it now." Her mother was wringing her small hands. "You can't mean that, darling. You mustn't even think of such a thing. Ronald——"

"Marcus will be here in a few minutes." Sophie put down the telephone. "You'd better lie down again, Cary. . . . Here, Bench, I'll have some brandy myself. . . . Now, Dorcas, there's only one possible course and that's to go straight through with this marriage. As Cary says, it's too late. We can't possibly change our plans. We can't postpone it, we can't do anything. Why, it wouldn't be possible even in this short time to telephone the guests—to do anything at all. Dorcas, you've got to pull yourself together and behave with dignity. You must."

"I won't marry. There'll be no wedding. You may as well get started on the guest list, Sophie. I'll do it myself. I'll do anything. But I won't marry the very day—the very day——"

"Look here, Dorcas, do you want everyone to say it was your fault? That you were unfair, that Ronald had some reason to kill himself? That you——"

"They'll say it anyway. Sophie, I can't—I can't—I won't——"

It resolved itself to that. All those reasons, all those arguments, even Cary's sobs and fluttering little hands had just then no meaning and no weight. She knew dimly that reason was on their side; that worldliness and prudence were on their side. And she huddled in a deep chair with her face in her hands and her throat aching horribly with sobs she would not, could not, free.

"I can't—I won't—I can't—I won't——"

It became her only answer. They were right. But she was right too; how could they understand that horrible, crushing sense of guilt? How could they understand that she must get away, go off by herself, be alone altogether—that she could not possibly, of all mad things, go on with that wedding? Walk in white satin down a church aisle while Ronald, because of her . . .

A long, sick shudder went over her. "I won't. . . ."

Cary, with a despairing look at the clock, cried: "Thank God, Marcus is coming."

He came. Fussily, energetically entering the room.

"What's all this? What's all this? Come now, Dorcas, you must be a brave girl——"

"Oh, Marcus, thank heaven you've come!" That was Cary. Sophie more coolly stood aside and explained.

"She says she won't be married today. We can't do anything with her."

"Not marry! Good God, Dorcas, you can't back out now."

"I won't—I can't——"

He was already dressed for the wedding; it was his place to give the bride away. Sole trustee and nearer the family than any relative, he had been the obvious choice. He was a tall man, gray haired and gray mustached, with light, worried blue eyes and deep bags under them. His morning coat was a marvel of tailoring; his neatly striped trousers impeccably creased. He carried a gold-handled cane and a silk hat and gloves which he put down on a chair as he came to Dorcas. He pulled the dressing table bench nearer her and sat down, puffing, and took her hands in his own.

"There are already reporters here," he said over his shoulder to Sophie. "Go down and tell them—tell them anything. No, wait." He frowned, holding Dorcas' hands tightly. "Tell them the family is grieved at the shocking and unexpected news of Mr Drew's suicide. Then they will ask if the wedding is to take place. You say, Sophie, this: 'The wedding will take place as arranged.' Say only that. Not a word more. They can make a column out of an adjective. . . . Now then, my dear . . ."

Sophie went quickly downstairs. The telephone rang and was ignored. Cary, wringing her small hands, cried: "Marcus, talk to her. Explain to her."

"Leave her to me, Cary. Now, Dorcas, my dear, I know how you feel. It's a horrible thing to have happened. Good God, if I had known he had any such idea in his mind I'd have put him under guard. At least until after the wedding. It's—it's hideous. It's a dreadful shock to you. But you mustn't hold yourself responsible. You——"

"But I am responsible. He did it because——"

"He did it because he was weak. Cowardly. Nobody is responsible for any other adult in the world. For your own sake, for Cary's sake, you've got to go on."

"I can't."

At eleven o'clock Sophie came back into the room; she carried a tray with black coffee and sandwiches on it. Cary by that time was walking up and down the rug, her pink chiffons trailing around her, the gold french clock clasped to her breast. Marcus, shouting, purple, was pacing, too, in circles around Dorcas.

Sophie, also, was dressed for the wedding. Beautifully, in brown with fur and a small, smart hat.

She put down the tray and took the clock from Cary's hands. "Go and get dressed," she said sternly to Cary. "Do you see this clock, Dorcas?"

"Won't you go away? Won't you leave me alone? . . . I'll talk to Jevan. I'll telephone now and ask him to forgive me —I'll do anything. Please leave me alone."

Marcus stopped abruptly in his pacing.

"Look here, Sophie," he said wearily. "I can't budge her. . . . Do you suppose—well, if she won't marry she won't. I'm willing to do everything in my power but I can't drag her to the altar."

"Dorcas is twenty-four," said Sophie. "After all . . ." She stopped, poured coffee and took the cup to Dorcas. "Drink this, Dorcas. Jevan has been on the telephone. Jevan as well as practically everybody we know," interpolated Sophie bitterly. "But Jevan——"

"Jevan. I must talk to him. I must explain. He'll understand."

"Oh, will he," said Sophie. "Well—you'll have a chance to talk to him, Dorcas. He's here."

Dorcas turned quickly. Jevan stood in the doorway. He came instantly into the room. He was dressed and ready for the wedding. What the well-dressed bridegroom will wear, he had thought grimly, hurrying, with young Willy Devany trying to help and getting in the way. Willy was waiting now —frantically, probably, watch in hand—at the church.

He looked at his own watch swiftly. He was tallish and rather well built; he had straight black eyebrows and a straight mouth which then looked angry. He was a little pale below brown skin but Dorcas didn't see that.

"Jevan—Jevan, I can't! Forgive me——"

Jevan's narrowed gray eyes—dark eyes with a spark of light in them—flickered once at Sophie and at Marcus. He jerked his chin toward the hall.

"I've done everything I can. I'm terribly sorry, my boy——"

"Thanks, Marcus. If you'll get out . . ."

"Why, by all means, Jevan. By all means."

Sophie, at the door, said: "It's ten after eleven."

Jevan himself closed the door. Closed it, looked at Dorcas and came to her. He sat down on the dressing table bench near her.

"Drink the coffee, Dorcas."

"Jevan, I must explain——"

"Drink it."

She did, one hot gulp after another. He got up, went to the tray and brought it back, placing it on the dressing table. There was another cup on the tray and he poured some coffee for himself, sugared it and took a sandwich.

"Jevan——"

"Finish your coffee."

She did that, too, helplessly, wearily. He ate several sandwiches. The little french clock ticked away on the table where Sophie had left it. The telephone buzzed again and stopped.

Dorcas put down her cup and leaned forward; she must explain, she must make him understand, he would understand.

He turned instantly.

"That's a good girl. Now then, Dorcas, get your clothes on."

"Oh no. You don't understand. I can't——"

"Hurry up."

There was a queer, quick little clutch at Dorcas' heart. He couldn't possibly mean to . . .

"Jevan, you've got to listen to me. Ronald did that because of me. It's all my fault. Last night——"

"It's a quarter after eleven. It will take at least twenty minutes to get to St Chrystofer's, maybe longer with the noon traffic. Hurry."

"I cannot marry. Not with Ronald——"

He got up. He seemed very tall. There was a flash back in his slate-gray eyes like lightning in a storm.

"There's no time for talk. Get dressed or, by God, I'll carry you down to the car as you are."

"Jevan——"

He gave a swift glance about the room and went to the mirrored doors of the long wardrobe and flung them open, one after the other, until he came to the wedding dress, hanging there with its train draped over it and the misty, floating white veil, incredibly crisp and lovely beside it.

He took both out and put them across the tumbled bed.

"Stand up." ·

"Jevan——"

He took her hands and pulled her on her feet. It wasn't any use trying to hold to the arms of the chair.

"Will you put on that dress or must I put it on you?"

"Please only listen. Let me explain——"

He went to the bell and put his thumb on it. Mamie came, panting, eyes bulging and worried.

"Put on Miss Dorcas' wedding gown. Hurry."

"But, Mr Locke——"

"Put it on her. I'll give you five minutes. Where are her stockings and slippers?"

"But, Mr Locke——" Mamie stopped short as he looked at her, said hurriedly: "In that drawer, sir. I'll get them."

"No—no," cried Dorcas.

He had his watch in his hand. He turned his back and walked over to a window and stood there looking down upon the gray, wind-swept world.

"Hurry up, Mamie," he said over his shoulder.

"The other foot, Miss Dorcas," said Mamie. "Let me get the seam straight."

There were mad, frantic possibilities. She could scream, she could struggle, but unfortunately Jevan was very much stronger than she. She saw herself nightmarishly being carried downstairs in her flannel housecoat and flat little bedroom slippers—being thrust into the car.

He meant it. There was no possible doubt of that.

Mamie, muttering, casting half-outraged, half-sympathetic, wholly frightened glances at Jevan's back, hurried. Her fingers flew. Stockings, little satin girdle. "Hurry, Miss Dorcas," whispered Mamie. White satin at last being slipped over her head and fastened. "Turn around, Miss Dorcas—there. Now your hair . . ."

"Make my bride beautiful, Mamie," said Jevan suddenly from the window, with something harsh and rough in his voice.

Going through the hall with Jevan's hand painfully tight on her arm, Dorcas had a glimpse of Cary's face, small, pale, but terribly thankful.

She thought of it—if she thought actually and with awareness of anything all the way to the church—with Jevan holding his watch in his hand and leaning forward, swearing, telling Grayson to hurry. Comparing his watch with the huge hands of the Chevrolet clock and frowning.

There was a small crowd around the church. There was a strip of red carpet. There was the sound of an organ—great, swelling tones which changed, just as a fluttering yellow cluster of bridesmaids surrounded her, into well-known, well-remembered, indescribably familiar and solemn tones.

Here was Marcus again. Jevan leaned above her, putting a white, fragrant bouquet in her hands. There were satin ribbons and the scent of gardenia. "I have no flower," he said. "May I have one from your bouquet?"

He waited an instant, dark eyes plunging into her own, then looked at her bouquet, broke off one delicate stalk of lily of the valley and vanished. Somebody turned her so she faced the church. Somebody—Marcus of course—put her gloved hand on his arm. There were people, swaying to look, rustling, silent as the measured peal of the organ became a march; there were yellow chiffon bridesmaids fluttering slowly ahead. There was the long church aisle and white ribbons and faces and away ahead a candle-lighted altar and a man robed in purple and white with a book in his hand amid massed yellow calla lilies.

And Jevan. She was all at once standing before that altar and Jevan had come from somewhere and was standing beside her. The music was softer; you could hear words—slow, solemn words. Deliberate words. Marcus Pett replied and stepped back. Jevan's shoulder touched her own; even if she turned and ran, stumbling in her train, he wouldn't let her go.

And she was to say something—repeat—but she couldn't speak.

Jevan, so only the bishop saw, put his hand upon her own so tightly it hurt and she repeated: "I, Dorcas Mary . . ." in a whisper.

Jevan's voice was low too. Everything was very still except the low, mellow tones from the organ which seemed to move quietly but almost tangibly about her.

There was a ring—Jevan's hands and the bishop's and her own—now they were putting it on, slipping it firmly on the bare finger, and she remembered Cary slitting that left glove and her small, intent face bent over the task. That was only yesterday.

They were to kneel. She did so, Jevan again beside her.

The prayer was short. Were they to stand now? Yes, only she couldn't. Jevan helped her. Jevan turned and took her hand firmly on his arm and great waves of melody swam about the church and lifted them out along the swelling tide, past faces, past bridesmaids, past everyone.

He was taking her swiftly through the vestibule. Willy Devany was holding the great outer door against the wind. His face was very white and he was crying, strangely and instead of congratulations, "Hurry—the car's waiting—hurry."

Grayson was at the door with the car. There were more faces, people along the sidewalk. Wind flapped the awning sharply over her head. Jevan gathered up her veil and she was in the car and a newsboy wriggled under somebody's arm and shouted: "News—news—all about . . ." and thrust a paper at them.

There were black headlines on that paper, too, and Dorcas saw them and they said: RONALD DREW MURDERED.

"Hurry, Grayson. Never mind the cops. Get going," cried Jevan and jumped into the car beside her.

He jerked down the rear shade and put his arm tightly, brusquely around her and pulled her close to him, so his mouth was at her cheek.

"Don't say anything," he said, watching Grayson. "The chauffeur will hear. I know you killed him."

CHAPTER 6

THE CAR MOVED smoothly and rapidly ahead and his arm held her so tightly against him that she couldn't move. In a queer little top layer of her mind which went right on thinking about the small surface things such as the rain against the car windows and Grayson's stiff neck and neat cap, and the long two-noted whistle of the traffic policeman at the corner—in that top layer she had an odd notion that if she spoke he would stop her, cover her mouth with his hand if need be.

It was, in that first instant or two, her only recognition of the thing. Ronald, said the newspapers, was murdered. It wasn't suicide, it was a murder. And Jevan had said he knew . . .

"*No, no, no*——"

"Stop that!" He thrust her back against the seat and leaned forward toward the dividing window, which was open. "How does this thing work?" He found the lever and turned it rapidly. A sheet of glass lifted smoothly between the driver's seat and the tonneau of the long, gliding car. He sat back again beside her, glanced at her once and said: "All right. He can't hear unless you have hysterics or something. Now listen, Dorcas. I know you killed Ronald. I don't blame you; he was a scoundrel and you—never mind that. I only want you to know——"

"I didn't kill him. He was alive when I left the apartment. He—he pushed the telephone off the table. He was alive——"

"Does anybody else know you were there?"

"No. Yes—that is, there was a doorman, I think. . . . You don't understand. I knew nothing of this. I——"

"The doorman! Did he know you? I mean, had you—had you been there often enough for him to know and recognize you?"

He wasn't looking at her now; he was watching the traffic ahead grimly, his mouth tight, his profile remote and enigmatic. There was a sweet heavy fragrance from her bouquet in her lap. Her satin train was over her knees, her white veil floating around her, obscuring her vision; there was the small sprig of lily of the valley in his buttonhole. His silk hat and gloves lay on the seat beside him. The car stopped for a traffic light and all around them other cars in the heavy noon traffic along Michigan stopped, too, and waited, engines throbbing, people inside the cars at either side of them turning to stare at a bride. Pavements glistened; lights glimmered palely from store windows; the traffic policemen in shining wet mackintoshes strove to direct that throbbing, pushing stream of cars and blew whistles frantically.

It was a world gone completely fantastic. In just twenty-four hours it had changed itself entirely, as if it had been overtaken by a new and strange dimension which distorted even familiar things—a well-known street, weather, faces she knew. And it wasn't a nightmare, for it was too real.

"Well—had you been there often?" said Jevan again, crisply.

"No. The doorman couldn't have recognized me. No one knew I was there." Too real; altogether too real, for it was happening and Ronald was murdered and she had been in his apartment just before that murder and the police would question her.

"I knew you were there," said Jevan. "I was there too. Later."

He paused but as she said nothing he went on swiftly: "You'd better know what I did."

The traffic policeman's whistle pealed weirdly through the rain and wind, through the hum and rush of tires and grinding of gears.

"You see, I got there just after you'd gone. In fact the cigarette was still smoking. I—well, I saw at once that he was dead. There was no question but that he died almost instantly. There was no use to call a doctor; I couldn't possibly have done anything for him. He must have died the moment the bullet—entered his forehead."

She was going to faint. For the first time in her healthy young life she was going to faint, for things all around her were dim and moving erratically out of focus and she felt very sick.

"Jevan!" It was a little, sick gasp. He heard and turned and took her quickly in his arms and put her head on his shoulder and rolled down the window beside him.

Dimly she knew he was fumbling with the veil over her face, finding the edge at last and pushing it back so fresh, cold air blew upon her face.

"You can't faint," he said sharply. "Listen, Dorcas. You can't. You've got to talk to me—there're only a few minutes to arrange everything."

His voice wavered in Dorcas' ears as humming blackness threatened to submerge it.

"Dorcas—Dorcas! Listen. You've got to pull yourself together. We've got to go through this day as if nothing had happened. Understand? You must do it!"

The compulsion in his voice reached her through those engulfing waves. His arms supported her; his cheek was against her head. Grayson saw it in the mirror but did not smile. He was too well trained and besides, that morning he was uneasy. He had seen the papers; the whole household knew of the trouble upstairs. But he knew, too, that young Mr Devany had been very queer and insistent about making sure that the car was exactly at the door the moment the ceremony was over; that young Mr Devany had been very nervous. And he, too, as they left the church had glimpsed the headlines.

Murder.

He looked quickly in the mirror again and away as quickly when he met Mr Locke's eyes. Involuntarily, under that look, he trod harder on the accelerator.

Dorcas felt the car gain in speed. Jevan was talking again, steadily and with sharp compulsion in his voice.

"I found Drew dead. I knew you had just gone. I—did everything I could. There was no use, as I said, to try to do anything for him. He was dead. Are you listening to me, Dorcas? Do you understand?"

Blackness was receding. She became more fully aware of his arms, holding her tightly but without warmth or tenderness.

"Answer me, Dorcas."

"Yes. Yes, I understand." Did she?

There was an instant's silence. His arms were tight and motionless. Then he said calmly: "Can you sit up now? Are you all right? . . . That's good."

She was sitting upright again; she had drawn away from him or his arms had neatly withdrawn and left her, now that she seemed no longer to need support. He searched her face and said tersely:

"It's only five minutes or so to the house and God knows what we'll find when we get there. And there's no telling when I'll get a chance to talk to you alone again. I want you to pay attention to me."

But there was something she must know. Everybody must know. Everybody in the world.

"Jevan, I didn't kill him. I know nothing about it. You must listen to me." Her voice, horrifyingly, was thin and frightened and unconvincing. It sounded to her own ears far away; as if somebody else was talking, protesting futilely.

His eyes went quickly away from her own. He glanced out the window; they were already at the lake and dark waves broke tumultuously against the white breakwaters.

"We are almost there. There'll be guests, hordes of peo-

ple. You must act as if nothing had happened. Understand
me? Go through with that reception and—and whatever
comes afterward as if you knew nothing at all of the murder. Don't try to think now. But do as I say. You——" He
turned then and looked at her briefly and said coolly: "Your
very life depends upon it, you know."

"Jevan——"

"When they question you, simply deny having been at his
apartment."

"But I——"

"Listen to me, Dorcas. I married you just now. You're my
wife. You must do this."

His wife. Dorcas Locke. But Ronald . . .

"But I didn't murder him. I know nothing of it."

A hard, taut little mask came over Jevan's brown face.

"All right," he said abruptly. "You know nothing of the
murder. But nevertheless, do as I say. Deny having been in
his apartment last night. Deny having seen him at all. And—
if you have a grain of courage, take your part this day as
gallantly as you can. If they give us time to prepare we may
think up some sort of plan—but they may not give us time."

They? Police? Oh, impossible!

"Deny everything," repeated Jevan. "If you don't know
what to say refuse to reply. If they know too much, if they
question you too much, refuse to answer and say you must
have your lawyer's advice. Understand me?"

Her lips moved numbly.

"Yes."

Again he shot a quick, dark look at her.

"I don't think you do," he said, shaking his head. "Good
God, rouse yourself. You look and act as if you were half
asleep. Don't you see the danger——"

The car stopped. Grayson was out, holding open the car
door. Immediately the house door was flung open and lights
poured out, only to lose themselves in the gray, diffuse light.
Wind and rain again on her face.

Jevan helped her out. At the door his grip on her arm
tightened and she felt him take a quick, short breath that
was like an exclamation. He leaned over her, shielding her
from the rain, and they ran up the steps and at the top he said
urgently: "Remember, Dorcas . . ."

There were lights in the hall and people. Bench, looking
pale and upset. Mamie, very red faced and crying. No guests

yet. Cary and Sophie and Marcus hadn't, of course, had time to arrive. But somebody was there already—several men who must be guests, yet they were not dressed for a wedding reception. Dorcas saw that and stopped. One of the men stepped forward and said: "Miss Whipple?"

She had an instant's clear glimpse of him—a slender, dark little man with a bored, sallow face and morose, heavy dark eyes. Two other men stepped forward, too, one at each side of the speaker, as if they were supporting him.

"Miss Whipple?" he said again. Mamie gave a sob in the background and cried: "Oh, Miss Dorcas, they've been everywhere. All over the house and in your room and——"

The little dark man glanced once at Mamie and said: "Shut up." Bench automatically closed the outside door. Jevan's arm went around Dorcas. The slender, dark man said: "You are Miss Whipple, aren't you?" as if some identification was necessary.

"Why—y-yes."

Jevan's arm pulled her backward a little so he seemed to interpose his own body between her and the advancing men.

"This is Mrs Locke," he said. "My wife. What is your business with her?"

There was an instant of complete and utter silence, an instant that hung suspended and static, capable of sharp, clear analysis. These men were intruders and they were dangerous. Their presence in that hall was a threat. Their observant, waiting eyes a menace. Even the hall—wide and silent, with its polished floors and its thin rugs, its bronze boy and its marble woman, its glimpses into other rooms of gilt chairs and flowers and a flower-banked mantel off in the drawing room at the right where the bride and wedding party were to receive—even the hall rejected the intruders. The whole silent house, waiting and empty as yet except of its own being, rejected them.

A man, uniformed and from the caterer's, scurried across the back of the hall, away back under the stair, casting a curious, sharp glance at them above the tray laden with silver. Off somewhere in the distance a violin wailed softly and was tuned. Another violin, and then a piano was struck in four clear little notes.

Over everything was the floating odor of coffee and of flowers. Dorcas' own flowers, held rigidly before her, sent up a soft warm fragrance of gardenias and lily of the valley.

It was an instant that engraved itself in clear, small lines upon her perceptions and, afterward, upon her memory so that the scent of gardenia was always to recall, not a visual memory of the lighted hall, the somber background of polished dark wood, the faces of three men all staring at her, but instead a sense of danger.

The dark little man was fumbling in a pocket of his brown tweed coat. He pulled out a paper, glanced at it and shoved it back into the pocket as if it didn't matter. He looked at Jevan and addressed him briefly:

"My name's Jacob Wait. I'm from headquarters."

"Well?"

"I've come here to investigate the murder of Ronald Drew."

"Investigate? What do you mean?"

"I mean I came to see Miss Dorcas Whipple." Jevan started to speak and the man Wait made a small, gentle gesture with one extraordinarily mobile and expressive hand. "All right," he said. "Mrs Locke. It doesn't matter. I have the proper authority if you want to see it."

"Why? Mrs Locke knows nothing of the murder."

"Mrs Locke," said Jacob Wait, "talked to Ronald Drew last night. I'm in a hurry. Do you want to answer my questions here, Mrs Locke, or would you prefer going to headquarters?"

"She'll talk to you here," said Jevan. "Here and now. Bench——"

"Yes sir."

"Where can we go——"

"Mr Whipple's study, sir. Wedding guests will be arriving shortly."

"Will you . . . ?" Jevan gestured briefly toward the narrow little passage that led off the main hall toward Penn Whipple's study.

In the distance the violins, joined now by a harp and a cello, began to play softly a Strauss waltz and the delicate melody floated along the passage around them.

The study was chilly and dark. Jevan turned on the lights. Wait and the two men with him, still supporting him like the wings of an army, followed them into the room. Jevan himself closed the door and shut out the light-footed, incongruously gay little melody.

"Now then," he said. "What do you want to ask my wife?"

CHAPTER 7

HIS WIFE. Well, she was that now. And she felt no different at all. But then the new dimension that had overtaken them pushed out normal feeling and thought; there was room only for horror, for catastrophe. He pulled a chair up for her—her father's great armchair. She sank down into it; her veil floated eerily around her and she put it back from her face and realized she was still carrying her bouquet and put that down on the shining mahogany table before her. Automatically, too, she stripped long white gloves from fingers that were heavy and lifeless. The man who had introduced himself as Jacob Wait, a name that for an instant seemed to have a slightly familiar ring, as if she'd heard it somewhere before, simply stood there at the other side of the table looking at her. The black leather of the great chair was cold and seemed damp to her touch. She leaned back in it, a slender figure in sheath-like white satin with silver slippers that barely touched the old Turkey-red rug. On the opposite wall a steel-engraved "Stag at Bay" stared blankly down and covered a clumsy, old-fashioned safe. All around the room bookshelves covered with glass reflected their figures weirdly in disjointed, shadowy sections. The room had been used very little since Pennyforth Whipple's death; was, in fact, rather avoided, and it had the indescribable air of desuetude such rooms take on with years.

Jacob Wait thrust his hands in his pockets and said: "You knew Ronald Drew?"

"Certainly she knew him. So did I. So did hundreds of other people." It was Jevan answering for her. Wait said abruptly: "I'm talking to Mrs Locke. Let her answer for herself. Did you know Ronald Drew, Mrs Locke?"

Mrs Locke? She moistened her lips and said: "Yes," almost inaudibly.

"How well did you know him?"

Jevan took a quick step forward and said: "See here, you can't——"

"I'll ask what I need to ask. Do you want to stay in the room?"

51

"Certainly."

"Then keep quiet. How well did you know Drew? Answer me, Mrs Locke."

How well had she known Ronald? The three faces—Wait's in the center—all three like searchlights, pinioning her with inquiry, waiting inexorably for her reply. Jevan moved over to stand beside her. And all at once she saw her danger.

Jevan had foreseen it. He had known it was to come and had warned her. She sought back frantically in her mind for the things he had told her to do. She was trapped; she had to fight for herself; no one else, now, could do it for her.

What had he said? Oh yes, deny. Deny everything. Deny . . .

"I knew Ronald Drew," she said in a small but fairly steady voice. "I don't know anything about his death."

"Wait blinked and one of the men beside him lifted thin sparse eyebrows as if in surprise. Jevan did not move. Wait said:

"You knew he was murdered?"

"Yes."

"Who told you?"

"It was in the paper. I saw the headlines."

"Do you know anything of the circumstances of the murder?"

"No."

Wait looked impatient. "Mrs Locke, you talked to Drew last night. We have the record of his telephone call to you at seven o'clock last night. It's the last telephone call he made. Why did he call you?"

Then they didn't know she had actually been in the apartment! Or did they know and were they merely trying to trap her into acknowledgment of it? Jevan had said deny; deny everything.

Instinctively, more frightened than she knew, she clung to it. Later there would be time to think, to reason, to seek a way out of the thing. Just now he had said to deny. But she'd have to admit to that telephone call if they had the record of it.

"Yes, he called me. He wanted to talk to me. He knew my wedding was today."

"What did he say?"

Jevan was so rigidly motionless that it was as if he had spoken a warning.

"He—he spoke of my approaching wedding. He wanted to say good-by to me."

"What else?"

"That's—that's all."

"How long did you talk?"

"Only a moment or two."

Again Wait made a little gesture of impatience.

"See here, Mrs Locke, we've been told that until your recent engagement Ronald Drew was your constant escort and that people were under the impression that you were to marry him. We've been told, too, that he was very much—ah —affected by your coming marriage to Mr Locke and that, in fact, when the news of his suicide came out the general impression was that he did it because of your marriage. Now there's no use in your evading the issue. Was he in love with you?"

"He—he said so. Yes."

"Did he ask you to marry him at any time?"

She couldn't look away from him; she tried to and failed.

"Y-yes. Yes, he did."

"And you refused?"

"Yes."

"How did he take your refusal? I mean, did he insist or did he——"

"Mrs Locke will answer all your questions, Wait, after she has seen her lawyer. She has a right——"

"Answer me, please, Mrs Locke."

"He—I—Jevan, what can I say?"

"Tell the truth, Mrs Locke. And I have a right to question her alone, Locke, if you want to leave."

"You need not answer, Dorcas——"

"She must answer." There was an ugly flash in the little man's eyes. He spoke to the man nearest him without turning his head. "If he says any more, put him out. . . . Now then, were you surprised when you heard, as the servants here tell me you did hear early this morning, that Drew had suicided?"

Dorcas' hands were clutching themselves together in her white satin lap. "I was horrified."

"But you thought he did it because of your marriage? Did you?"

"I—yes. Yes, I was afraid of it."

"Why?"

"Because I—because he had threatened——"

"Oh, he'd threatened to commit suicide if you married Locke?"

"Y-yes. That is, I didn't think he meant it."

"And when you heard of his death you refused at first to go through with the wedding? Don't lie to me, I've questioned your servants. They've told me of his visits here—yes, and of the pressure brought to bear upon you to bring about your wedding to Locke here——"

"That's enough. Get out. All of you. You can't——" Jevan was standing over Wait, his eyes blazing from his white face, his hands doubled into hard fists.

Wait didn't move, although the two men with him moved up closer quickly. Wait said amicably: "All right, all right, Locke. Keep your shirt on. But tell your wife to answer my questions. We know too much for you to try to dodge them. Drew was murdered and somebody killed him."

"My wife knows nothing at all about it. You have no right——"

"I have every right," snapped Wait, his suave affability vanishing. "I have every right. Ronald Drew was murdered last night. About eight or a little after a woman was in his apartment. I want to know who the woman was. About nine-thirty a man was in his apartment. I want to know who that man was. I've already inquired about Mrs Locke—the servants say she went to bed about eight. I've not inquired about you, Locke. What about it? What did you do last night and where were you?"

"I was at my club. Any number of men saw me. You can easily establish that."

"What time did you leave?"

"I'm not sure. Between nine-thirty and ten, I think. I was with Willy Devany."

"Where did you go?"

"Home, of course."

"What time did you arrive there?"

"I don't know exactly. Devany brought me in his car; we sat out in front and talked a little. He might know what time it was."

"You mean young Willy Devany, of the Devany Packing Company?"

"Yes. He was my best man today."

"And you were in his company from the time you. left the club till you got home?"

"Certainly. What is this? Do you think I shot Drew?"

Something became fixed in Wait's morose eyes. "Oh, so you knew he was shot?"

"Certainly. It was in the papers. But how do you know he was murdered? Why did the papers first say suicide and later murder? Are you sure it wasn't suicide——"

"I'm sure," said Wait and spoke to one of the men with him. "Take the name of Locke's club and names of the men he claims saw him there."

"Check them?"

"No. I'll do it myself."

"Okay." A notebook was in the plain-clothes man's hands and he moved to Jevan's side and began to question in a lowered, husky voice, and to write.

Wait turned back to Dorcas. "Now then, Mrs Locke, when Drew talked to you last night did he say anything of his immediate plans?"

"No."

"Did he make any kind of threat?"

"Threat——"

Jevan interrupted.

"Dorcas, this has gone far enough! Refuse to answer——"

"Did he threaten to do anything to stop the wedding? Had he," said Wait in a matter-of-fact way, "any kind of hold over you?"

"Don't answer, Dorcas." Jevan was at her side again, bending close over her, making her meet his eyes. "Don't answer."

"I must answer." She looked at the detective. "No! He made no threats! He had no hold whatever over me. There was nothing—nothing he could have done. He had wanted to marry me, yes. He urged me, even, to marry him. But that was all. There was nothing he could have used as a—a threat."

Jevan dropped her hands and stood straight again and looked, too, at the detective. There was something triumphant in that look, as if he'd scored a victory. He said, almost smiling, except it was a queer, tight smile: "Well, there you are, Mr Detective. Satisfied now, are you?"

"No. Except that you've coached your wife. However

. . ." He paused thoughtfully. Away off in the distance
doors were opening and closing; there was a murmur and
hum of motion and voices from the main part of the house.
The guests were arriving, turning out in full numbers in order to show their support. Behave as if nothing at all had
happened. It was like a motto. But tomorrow, that night even,
Chicago would rock with it.

Jevan said suddenly: "The guests are arriving. If you could
postpone your inquiry . . . ?"

Unexpectedly Wait seemed to agree. "Why not?" he said.
"I'll see you later."

"We are going on a wedding trip," said Jevan. "We leave
immediately after the reception."

"Cancel the trip," said Wait simply and looked at
his watch.

"Cancel—look here, Wait. What do you mean by that? Are
we under arrest?"

"No."

"Then you can't prevent us leaving."

"Oh, can't I," said Wait. "Try it and see." He turned and
walked to the door. Dorcas leaned forward, clutching the
slippery arms of the chair. Was he actually going, leaving
them? At the door he turned. "I'm giving you a break," he
said abruptly. "I could detain you for questioning until your
wedding party was all over. That'd look nice in headlines,
wouldn't it! Bride and groom not present owing to being involved in a murder inquiry. Well, I'm not doing it. But I'll
be back. And don't leave town. I can get an order to stop you
if I have to. That'd look nice in headlines too. Well, I
won't do that either—but don't try to leave. Miss Whipple,
do you have a green suit?"

It was altogether unexpected and was exactly like a blow.
Dorcas almost staggered with the impact of it. A green suit
. . . the doorman . . . and Mamie had said they'd been all
over the house, looking . . . searching for what? For a
green suit? But the doorman . . . He'd had only a
glimpse . . .

Jevan was speaking. He was saying agreeably, too smoothly
perhaps, "Of course she might have a green suit. Or a blue
or yellow one. Why not?"

If Wait heard Jevan there was no evidence of it, for he was
looking at Dorcas. Quietly, almost as if he were thinking

of something else, yet Dorcas, meeting his eyes helplessly, felt guilt in her own. In another moment he would ask her point-blank if she had been in Ronald's apartment, or perhaps he knew already. Certainly he had questioned the servants about what she had done the previous night. Then he suspected her. Why? Definitely and specifically because he knew she had been with Ronald? Or merely in a general way because she was one of Ronald's associates?

His eyes were extraordinarily discerning. She was assailed by an uneasy notion that he could read her thoughts. But he said finally, rather affably: "How about it, Mrs Locke?"

Probably, helplessly, she would have replied but the door into the hall flung open and Sophie entered hurriedly. Her handsome brown gown was unruffled, her small hat at exactly the smart angle, her sables beautiful and soft over her shoulders. Her eyes were very quick and Dorcas knew at once that Sophie realized exactly what was happening.

She said, however, calmly: "Oh, there you are, Dorcas. Guests are here. You must receive them——"

"Who are you?" said Wait neatly.

Her eyes flashed once but she did not resent the question or show surprise.

"You are the police," she said. "I knew, of course, that you were here about poor Ronald's suicide. I am Mrs Thomas Whipple. Won't you let Mrs Locke go now? It's her wedding——"

Sophie's pleasant voice had never been more tactfully restrained yet charming. Wait, however, looked very bored. He said: "You live here?"

"Yes."

"We were talking of Mrs Locke's green suit. It has a long coat and a collar of reddish fur. A high collar. I'd like to see it, please."

There was no way to warn Sophie. They could only listen and watch to see whether she showed recognition of the suit and offered to bring it to the detective, as naturally she would do.

In an instant's flash of memory Dorcas thought back to the fatally observant doorman. She had seen nothing of him, had been conscious of him only as a dark, suitably uniformed figure, opening the car door and vanishing; unimportant, of no significance whatever. Yet he had seen what she wore, had noted it so exactly that the detective had now this terrifyingly accurate description of it. Had he seen her face? Could he identify her?

Jevan made a motion to speak. But Sophie was replying smoothly, without a flicker of her thin white eyelids:

"Mrs Locke has no such suit as the one you describe. At least I can't remember it. Do you possess such a suit, Dorcas?"

She said it coolly and looked at Dorcas and the wary, communicative look in her hazel eyes reminded Dorcas that, in truth, she had given the thing to Sophie.

But the detective did not wait to question her further. He looked at his watch, said briefly: "It really doesn't matter. The woman who wore the green suit was seen and can be identified," and walked out of the room—lightly, exactly like a cat. The two men with him jerked around, as if his action had taken them by surprise, and then followed him, their footsteps heavy on the thin rugs and polished old floors where Jacob Wait's had been almost inaudible. Through the open door came distant strains of a popular dance tune, light and soft with delicately marked rhythm, "She shall have music . . . wherever she goes. . . ."

Sophie put out a smartly gloved hand and closed the door.

"Pray heaven they don't get hold of Cary," she said coolly. "Don't tell me now, Dorcas; there isn't time. Although what that green tweed suit of yours has to do with the police! Of course they were questioning you about Ronald?"

"Yes." Jevan got out his handkerchief and wiped his forehead.

"So it was murder," said Sophie. "Well . . . Dorcas, you must get out there. Behave as if nothing had occurred. Here, let me fix your veil. You look like death."

Jevan was staring rather grimly at the blank, dark panels of the door.

"How did they know it was murder?" he said. "I can't remember anything——" He stopped abruptly. Sophie gave a last touch to Dorcas' veil and handed her her gloves and opened the door.

In the hall, facing them, was another large, gilt-framed mirror and again Dorcas saw her white image advancing mistily in it. Jevan was beside her, Sophie at one side. The gay little dance tune floated around them. ". . . She shall go marching . . . to honeymoon time. . . ."

Dorcas thought of the mirrors in Ronald's apartment; so many of them that they had seemed to store up a secret record of their own. Had they, she wondered, stored up also her own reflection to reveal at their will? But she hadn't murdered Ronald. Who, then, had?

CHAPTER 8

THE WEDDING RECEPTION was actually a success. Its success, however, was due to really heroic heights of habit and convention attained not only by those most directly concerned but also by the guests. Probably there was not a soul there who did not know, or did not learn within five minutes of his arrival, about the murder. There had been the papers as they came out of church; the news had gone like quicksilver—whispered, speculated upon in italics. But once in the Whipple house there was an instant agreement, the more loyal for its being unspoken, the more friendly for its being so desperately needed by Dorcas and her mother, to behave exactly as if nothing had occurred. Support Cary Whipple. Support Dorcas. Indicate by no glance, no whispered word, no hint of sympathy, even, that there was a murder.

There was, however, a feverishness about the determined gayety of the afternoon. Excitement ran like a darting, taut little thread everywhere through the crowded, brilliantly lighted rooms.

Furs and faint perfumes and flowers and faces. Gloved hands and murmured words and faces. Silks and morning coats and faces. Music always in the background and now and then the yellow chiffon of some bridesmaid flashing somewhere through the moving, overlapping circles. And faces. All of them kind, all of them producing complimentary, pleasant words, all of them reserving a secret thought. Ronald Drew was murdered; is there something back of this?

Afterward the thing resolved itself in Dorcas' memory to a series of pictures. Herself in heavy white satin, her train curving in heavy, shimmering bluish folds below, her white veil flung back. Her mother in gray chiffons and a spray of orchids, smiling a little tautly, a little desperately, altogether gallantly. Conventions are made for emergencies; it was one of the rules Cary Whipple had impressed upon Dorcas all her life and now that it was an emergency and a dreadful one Cary had quite simply resorted to a rule.

Marcus Pett, beaming falsely, anxiously hovering over Cary, retiring now and then to the dining room and coming back with his face successively more and more flushed and the flustered anxiety in his eyes more and more apparent.

More people; more music; the soft clatter of cups and glasses from the huge dining room, unused as a rule, for the three women usually had their meals in a small and friendlier sunroom at the back of the house. Dancing, too, in the library with the rugs removed, leaving bare and perilously polished floors. The scent of gardenias. The heat in the rooms; the sense of the front door continually opening and closing.

And Jevan always beside her. Talking. Fending off prolonged conversations.

It went on and on; sometime the little receiving line dissolved, leaving the flower-banked fireplace. Dorcas found herself in a chair with a plate and cup in her hand.

It was desperately hot. Surely the people were thinning. Anyway, it would soon be time to dress for the train. But they were not to go away!

"Dorcas——"

It was Willy Devany, bowing, taking her hand.

"I'm late," he said and bent and kissed her cheek lightly. "Good wishes, my dear."

He was as usual perfectly turned out and as usual he looked thin and pale and extremely unimportant. Years ago at dancing school, clad in the ridiculously affected clothes his mother insisted upon, he had bowed to her exactly the same way, a little diffidently, a little shyly, a little uncertainly, as if he knew beforehand that he would step on her little pumps and guide her into other dancers.

There was now something a little wistful in his pale blue eyes as he kissed Dorcas.

"Good wishes," he said again. "Where's Jevan? . . . Oh, there you are." Jevan was beside her at once. Curious how he'd managed all that afternoon to be close beside her when anyone lingered to talk to her and it was necessary for her to reply at length.

"Congratulations."

"Thanks, Willy."

Willy touched his collar, moved his elbows uneasily in his smoothly tailored coat and sent a hunted blue glance about them before he leaned toward Jevan and said: "You've seen the——"

"Yes. They were here when we got back from the church."

"Oh. Then they know——"

"I'm afraid so."

"My God," said Willy in a desperate kind of whisper. "My God." His small fair face looked white and worried again as it had looked when he held the door for them at the church.

"They were here," said Jevan. "They'll probably be around to you to substantiate my alibi."

"Oh, my God," said Willy again hopelessly. "How did they know? Was there—evidence?"

Jevan shrugged a little. "I don't know. Mere supposition, I think. No evidence unless somebody saw——"

Somebody—that meant the doorman. And evidence? What did he mean by evidence? Fingerprints and things like that? Had she left fingerprints? Had she left traces of having been in the apartment other than those intangible traces in the mirror's records? Fingerprints—good heavens, the glass of whisky and soda! The mirrored cigarette box; had she touched it? Her cigarette. But fingerprints couldn't be taken from a cigarette. Or could they? The door then—what else?

Willy was talking.

"But good God, Jevan, how did they know it was murder? What was left? What did you——"

"I don't know. Something."

Somebody came and joined the little group; somebody else drifted to them. Presently Willy was gone.

And it was time to dress for the train. Sophie said so, and Cary.

"But we aren't," began Dorcas helplessly and Jevan again was at her side and fending it off.

"Right you are, Mother Cary," he said and Cary blushed a little and smiled, though the fixed bright look of determination in her lovely blue eyes did not relax. "Come, Dorcas," he said.

But before they went upstairs they danced. Around the full circle of the huge library with Jevan's arm holding her tight against him. Somebody held her bouquet and she clutched her train in her left hand and Jevan danced smoothly and they moved as evenly and rhythmically as if they had been of one piece. This way, that way, her soft veil floating backward, her silver slippers light. Her head was on a level with his shoulder and so close to it she could have leaned her head upon it. Once she looked up and he was looking down at her.

The look held her, plunging down into her own for a significant moment as if he said things to her and, actually, as if she replied. Then he smiled a little and his eyes became merely pleasant and friendly and he said briskly: "Nice music, isn't it? You dance very well, Dorcas. Remember dancing school and Mademoiselle?"

She did remember. Mademoiselle always had a cold and suffered from chilblains and was like a feather once she started to dance.

". . . if you can imagine," said Dorcas, finishing the thought aloud, "a feather in tight black curls and black wool dress."

". . . and thick black stockings. I'm proud of you, Dorcas; I didn't realize you had so much stamina. Or Cary either, for that matter. . . . Let's dance around again. The orchestra will do an encore."

They did, smiling because it was the bride and groom, because they were a handsome, well-mated couple, because it was a wedding, because their day's work was nearly done, because they were well paid, because there was hot mulled wine and Tom and Jerrys and huge plates of sandwiches and salad waiting for them at Cary's express order; they prolonged the soft dance tune to a lingering pause.

As the music stopped somebody said: "Have you kissed the bride yet, Jevan?"

"Of course he has," cried one of the bridesmaids. "In the car."

Jevan looked down at Dorcas; he was laughing softly but there was a little gleam away back in his eyes. "I'll kiss her again," he said and put his hand under Dorcas' chin and lifted her face and kissed her mouth. It was a firm, deliberate kiss, his mouth warm. Ronald's face flashed dreadfully across Dorcas' memory and she pulled sharply away. Jevan's hand dropped instantly.

"It's time to go," he said abruptly, his mouth now rather tight and grim.

Through people again, up the broad, gleaming stairway. Halfway up someone cried, laughing: "Your bouquet, Dorcas," and she remembered and stopped and tossed the bouquet lightly into the laughing flutter of bridesmaids below. There was a scramble and a shriek. "Ann got it. Ann Watson. Oh, Ann, when?"

Then they were beyond the turn of the stairs. Away below was the hubbub of voices, of departing cars, of the front door constantly opening.

Upstairs it was rather quiet and a little cool after the heat of the rooms below.

Mamie met them.

"I've fixed the guest suite," she said. "Miss Sophie told me you wouldn't be leaving."

She ushered them into it. There was a fire, flowers on the table, heavy curtains drawn against the sleet and wind and gathering darkness.

Jevan closed the door.

"It's just as well to stay here," he said. "I was thinking vaguely of a suite in some hotel; this is better. Sit down, Dorcas. I'll have Mamie bring you something to eat. You scarcely tasted anything."

He pulled a deep, cushioned chair up to the fire. The big rooms, two of them connecting, with a huge and rather cold bathroom and dressing room between, had been aired hurriedly and warmed but there was still the faint scent of lavender and old wood which rooms acquire when they've been unused for a long time. They were not unpleasant rooms, almost exactly alike in mahogany and damask, gilded light brackets and thick carpets, plate-glass mirrors and deep chairs.

She sat down. She must have sighed, for he glanced at her and came to her and said: "I'll help you with that veil."

The little circle of twisted satin holding the lace cap in place had been tighter than she realized. He removed it, putting it on the table so the delicate folds of white hung across the polished, massive old mahogany with a strange, almost eerie incongruity. She sighed again and pushed her hair back from her forehead. She looked very small and very pale and a little frightened above her satin finery.

"And that," she said with a little laugh that caught in her throat, "is my wedding. Police at the door . . . murder . . ."

Her head was heavy and tired. She put her face in her hands.

The room was very still except for the small hiss of gas and the swish of wind and rain—or was it now sleet?—against the windows. Jevan seemed to move toward her and then stopped abruptly and went to the bell and put his thumb on it.

"I'll have Mamie bring food," he said. "There's no need in a prolonged family dinner tonight. Your mother ought to be sent to bed anyway. . . . And I'll have my bags sent here. They're at the station, I think, in the checkroom. The guests are leaving and I—I think we've got to have a talk, Dorcas. Before the detective returns."

Mamie came to the door and he gave brief directions. Then he closed the door again and came back to her, pulled a chair up near the fire, sat down and took out a cigarette case.

"Cigarette?"

She shook her head. Thinking again, with terrifying clearness, of the night before, of Ronald and the cigarette he'd given her and—what had she done with that cigarette? She tried again desperately to remember and couldn't. But Jevan had said something about a cigarette. What? She sought back for it, groped for an obscure significance that had seemed to attach itself somehow to whatever it was Jevan had said and failed to recall either. For Jevan was talking, and she must listen.

"Now then, Dorcas. I hate to make you talk of it now. But I've got to get things clear. You see . . ." He paused and watched a wisp of smoke drift lightly toward her and went on: "You see, I know you were there in his apartment. I was there only a little later. Your cigarette was still smoking and I put it out. I wiped off the glass that you had used. There are no fingerprints there. I wiped the door where you might have touched it and also where I touched it myself. I disposed of the cigarette you had smoked. And I—I took the revolver where you—where it had dropped there by the sofa and I wiped it, too, with my handkerchief so as to leave no fingerprints."

His voice was rough suddenly, as if he forced himself to speak. He was frowning, scrutinizing his cigarette absorbedly.

"But I . . ." she began and again fumbled vaguely about the matter of the cigarette, again failed to discover whatever significance it seemed obscurely to have, and he went on, cutting into her denial.

"Then I—I picked up his hand and—put his own fingerprints on the revolver and left it there beside him."

"Jevan——"

"Yes. So you see, I thought I got everything. But I must have missed something. Tell me, what did I miss? What evidence do they have against you?"

"I didn't kill him, I told you that. I was there but——"

He looked at her again, quickly and keenly; suddenly he tossed his cigarette into the grate and got up and went to her and took her hands.

"Look at me, Dorcas. Say that again. Tell me the truth." He paused and then said more gently: "It doesn't matter. He —he wasn't worth good lead. But I must know. You're my wife, you know."

Something in his eyes questioned her more deeply and more poignantly than his words. He waited and she didn't reply because again, horribly, Ronald's flushed face and bright eyes—Ronald as she had seen him last—came between them.

Jevan's face stiffened a little. He said again but in a different voice, a little grimly, a little dryly, "You're my wife, you know. I can't have you charged with murder. But I must know the truth."

CHAPTER 9

SLEET SWISHED against the windows. Little blue and red points of flame hissed gently. Below, the great door was opening, closing—opening, closing. Cars were departing thickly now and there was the soft throb of engines and the murmur of low gears, blurred by the wind and sleet.

Jevan would stand by her.

He would know what to do and would do it; without questioning she accepted that.

Well, then she'd better tell him.

So she did, briefly; making it a bald, bare little recital with no attempt to justify either her own impulse or her own failure adequately to meet the situation Ronald had thrust upon her.

Midway in her story Jevan got up and prowled about the room, winding up at a window where he pulled the curtain aside and stared out into the storm and darkness while her small voice went on and on, threading its way among the spaces of the big, quiet room, threading its way, too, through the ugly little tale—ugly and, now, touched with the macabre.

Stripped of every possible word, it did not make a fine story. Wouldn't have made that in any event, for she did not come out of it with flying colors.

". . . and then the telephone rang," she said. "And when he went to answer it I—went away. There was a taxi at the corner of Lake Shore Drive and I took it and came home."

Jevan waited a moment as if she had not yet finished and then said rather roughly: "Is that all?"

She nodded, staring at the fire. Downstairs, during her barren, unadorned little tale, the continual opening and closing of the door and the throbbing rhythm of departing cars had gradually died away.

Jevan let the curtain drop, went to the table and took a cigarette from a box there, lighted it and without a glance at Dorcas went to the fireplace and put his elbow on the mantel. He seemed very tall to Dorcas, looking up at him from her deep chair. The little points of light made a glow on his face but she could read nothing in his expression. The cigarette was half finished before he spoke. He said then:

"I'll have to ask you some questions."

"I've told you everything."

"Yes, I know. But—well, first I think we'd better get this straight. It will simplify things. Did you love Ronald?"

Had she? His voice demanded complete honesty.

"I don't know. I suppose I thought I did—or I felt sorry for him. But—but now—I don't know. Last night——"

"Well?" The word was short and sharp and still he didn't look at her.

"Oh, I don't know. I was confused. I——"

"Did you consider eloping with him as he suggested?"

"No."

"Why not?"

"I—couldn't."

"Why?"

"Because——"

"Well?"

"Oh, I couldn't," she cried, throwing out her hands in a desperate little gesture which was like a plea for mercy. He said nothing and she cast about in her mind for reasons and there were many. "The wedding was all arranged. I couldn't let my mother down like that. Or—or you."

This time his eyes flickered her way quickly, lingered for an instant and then went back to the fire.

"Oh, I see. The wedding was arranged and, after all, you did have a nice picture of yourself going down the aisle in white satin and all your bridesmaids around you. And you didn't want to let your mother down. Yes, I see. That would have been difficult. Otherwise you might have considered Ronald's neat suggestion. Is that right?"

"No! No; you are unfair. I—there wasn't time to analyze. You have no right to question me!"

"Oh, don't I!" He threw away the cigarette and turned abruptly and came to stand over her. He looked angry; there was a flash of smothered violence in his eyes. "Don't I! You're my wife. I have a right to ask if you were in love with another man. If you're still in love with him——"

"Poor Ronald," said Dorcas unexpectedly. "He's dead——"

"That doesn't matter. Listen to me. When he made love to you——"

"Don't. I've told you because I—I thought you'd help me."

"Yes, I know that's why you told me. Sheer instinct for self-preservation on your part. And it hurts you to be questioned but I'm going to continue to be a brute and ask you questions. When Ronald made love to you—even then didn't you weaken? Didn't you forget even for an instant the fine wedding that was planned? Didn't you just for a moment, in his arms," said Jevan coolly, "forget your handsome wedding?"

"*Don't*," she cried again sharply and put her face in her hands.

He waited and as she didn't answer he said more gently: "Are you grieving for Ronald? Is that it?"

"No. No, I—oh, please don't. I'm tired. This is horrible. His murder—who could have done it? Who could have murdered him? Why? He had no enemies. . . ."

She felt Jevan turn again and walk away to stand before the fire. He said presently: "Who indeed? I suppose we'd better consider that, hadn't we? After all, to keep our own heads out of the noose ought to be our first consideration. If we succeed in doing that there'll be plenty of time later for —other things. Who did murder Ronald? Try to remember everything, Dorcas. . . . Was there anything at all during the time of your—visit—in his apartment that struck you as being a little out of the ordinary? Unusual in any way, I mean. Even in his behavior or in anything he said?"

She thought back wearily; she had told him everything. "There was my impression that—that there was whispering in the kitchen. It was only an impression. And again I had the feeling that there was something in the apartment—someone besides us. It—there was no reason for my feeling. I saw no one. Except the door moved——"

He whirled around. "You didn't tell me that. What about the door? What do you mean?"

She told him; there wasn't much to tell because it was so slight an impression. He frowned into space and did not comment and she went on to another dimly noted, vaguely remembered circumstance. "And there was a car. A car passed us when we left the house. It went slowly and when I returned later there was a car just leaving. At least I had an impression it was just leaving. There was a car, too, just behind us when we drove up to the apartment house. That's why the doorman left so quickly—I thought he left us before he could possibly have seen me."

He did not seem interested in the car but he roused to question her at length about the doorman. About the telephone. Ronald had thrust it over the edge of the table, had he? It had fallen on the floor? Had Ronald answered it? She didn't know.

"Is there nothing else, Dorcas? Think."

"Nothing."

"Where's the nearest telephone? Is there one upstairs? I don't want anyone to overhear."

"In my room. I'll show you——"

"Never mind. I know."

The door closed behind him. Downstairs all was silent. She thought of the empty, lighted rooms, servants clearing away. Sleet and wind and darkness outside. Away off in town Ronald's apartment was dark now too. With the mirrors veiled and empty.

Who had murdered him? What motive could anyone have had?

The little sigh of the gas flames filled the room gently, soothingly. She put her head back against the chair. There was no use thinking.

Mamie knocked and came into the room.

"I'll fix the table for your dinner, if you please, Miss Dorcas. Mr Jevan said——"

"Yes, Mamie."

She had brought a small lace cloth, napkins, a tray of silver.

"Your mother's gone to bed," she volunteered. "Mr Pett talked to her a long time; he was real sensible; made her feel better. I think she's going to rest now."

"That's good."

"Yes, Miss Dorcas. Is there anything——"

"No, thank you, Mamie."

Jevan came into the room again with the evening paper, still rolled and wet, under his arm.

"That's right, Mamie," he said, unrolled the paper and spread it out flat on a footstool near the fire. Dorcas' eyes went to the headlines as if magnetized.

"It's all here," said Jevan, reading. "They've been rather kind on the whole. Not a mention of your name. No evidence, no implication at all, in fact. Something about this man Wait—says he's new to the Chicago detective force, came here from Wrexe County recently. Oh, here we are. . . ." He stopped abruptly to read some particular paragraph over and over again slowly, frowning as he did so. Mamie went quietly away. And presently, without further comment he gave the paper to Dorcas and sat there smoking, looking thoughtfully at the fire.

She shrank from it and yet must read it. The account, as Jevan said, did not even hint at her own implication in the affair. What was the paragraph he had read and reread so intently?

There were pictures accompanying it: Ronald, handsome

face in profile; photographs of the apartment—one of a room with deep, modern white furniture and mirrors, a room that was dreadfully familiar. She searched it, holding her breath, driven by a horrible need, for evidences of her own presence. There was the divan, there the table, there the white paneled door. He'd been murdered, then, in that very room. And Jevan had said her cigarette was still smoking when he arrived.

The telephone was on the floor. She sought for it, too, and found it in a tangle of wires at the base of the table. Below the picture was a paragraph: ". . . telephone flung to the floor was one of the reasons, Mr Wait admits, which led to his conclusion that the death of the socially prominent young man was not suicide as was at first reported. An autopsy leads the police to believe the murder was committed between nine o'clock and midnight. Fingerprints on the revolver were found to be those of the dead man but were so smudged and in such a position on the revolver that the police believe they were placed there deliberately by the murderer. Mr Wait refused to be interviewed at length but did say that the whole setup looked 'phony' and that the position of the telephone on the floor indicated either that some kind of struggle took place previous to the murder or that Mr Drew was endeavoring to summon help when the fatal shot occurred."

"There's no mention of a woman in a green suit," said Jevan abruptly.

Dorcas looked up quickly; he was watching her, waiting for her to finish reading.

"No."

"No mention of the man who came later—that's me—no mention of the doorman. Looks very much as if Wait's news items were hand-picked by Wait. As if his real evidence is being kept secret."

Slowly she put down the paper. The photograph of the room in Ronald's apartment was uppermost and she turned it over, face downward on the carpet, so she could no longer see it.

"You've asked me questions," she said. "I have two to ask."

"Very well. I know one of them: What was I doing in Ronald's apartment? That's it, isn't it? I see it is. Well . . ." He leaned forward, putting his elbows on his knees and looking straight at her. "Suppose I don't answer it?"

"Why won't you answer?"

"I'll answer the question behind it. I didn't murder Ronald. He's small loss; I don't think it would trouble my conscience much if I had. But I didn't. Now your other question."

She leaned forward this time, linking her hands despairingly upon her slender, satin-covered knee.

"Do you believe I murdered him?"

He looked at her quickly, looked away, waited at least a moment before replying and then said: "I don't care."

"You——"

"I don't care. He was . . ." He hesitated. A note of something chill and hard came into his voice. "He was thoroughly rotten. He needed shooting. I don't care whether you killed him or not. What I want to know—what I must know—is something else. Something that concerns only——"

There was a knock at the door. Jevan listened, got up as if rather thankful for the interruption than otherwise and went to the door. It was Sophie. Jevan pulled up a chair for her, too, and she sank into it wearily.

"The legs," she said, "are exhausted. I've walked a thousand miles today and old Mrs Mortimer dug one of her sharp heels into my instep. Everything all right, Dorcas? I told Mamie to fix these rooms. A reporter was on the telephone just now; said they understood your wedding trip was postponed and wanted the rumor confirmed. I told him there was no change in your plans at all. He didn't believe me of course. Said he'd found that your reservations had been made for today and were not canceled but that you didn't leave." She sighed.

"What did you say?" asked Jevan.

"There wasn't anything to say. I repeated, said there was no change in your plans and hung up. And I hadn't more than put down the receiver when another one called and said the same things except he—well," said Sophie reluctantly, "he had whatever it took to ask if the delay in your departure wasn't due to the Drew murder investigation. I said no and hung up again. But God knows what the papers will have. The second one was from the Call. And you know what that means."

Dorcas felt herself cringe. She did know what it meant. The Call specialized in love nests and murder was an added fillip.

Jevan said coolly: "There's bound to be a certain amount of that kind of thing. Can't be avoided."

"Sophie, you were grand about that suit," said Dorcas wearily. "The policemen were questioning——"

Sophie glanced at her once discerningly, accepted a cigarette and a light from Jevan and said, puffing for the light: "Good heavens, Dorcas, I knew you went to see Ronald. At least, I—well, when I took the suit to my own room this morning (she gave it to me last night, Jevan) I saw it was damp—knew you'd been out. Guessed it was to meet Ronald. Guessed—well, to tell the absolute truth, Dorcas, I had rather hoped you would manage to see Ronald before your wedding. Now don't look at me like that, Jevan. It was only fair to Dorcas and fair to Ronald. I—well, I'm a little sentimental. And I did think we'd all been a little hard on Ronald. I even went so far as to hint to Dorcas it wouldn't be a bad idea to see him."

"What did you expect to come of such a meeting?" inquired Jevan.

Sophie shrugged. "Nothing. Dorcas wasn't in love with Ronald. I thought—if I thought anything, really—it was a good time for her to discover it. But don't credit me with sensible and psychological motives, for mainly I only wanted her to arrange somehow to see him if she wanted to. That's all. And I'm sorry. Good God," said Sophie, her smile vanishing so that all at once her pretty, well-bred face was pale and drawn. "Good God, I never dreamed of anything like this. Dorcas, did you—that is, could you——"

"Dorcas didn't murder him, if that's what you're trying to say," said Jevan shortly.

"Oh," said Sophie. "Well, that's good. So long as the police don't think she did! Did they know you were there, Dorcas? Is that why they came——"

"No," said Jevan. "They only knew that she had talked to him last night. They had a record of the telephone call he made to the number here. That's all."

"Oh," said Sophie again. "Thank heaven for that. Did anybody see you entering or leaving the apartment?"

Dorcas did not reply, for just then someone came along the hall rather quietly. Jevan had not closed the door and yet so heavily carpeted was the wide hall that they did not hear Marcus' footsteps until he reached the door. Were not, in fact, aware of his presence there until Dorcas became suddenly conscious of a lightish patch of something looming in the shadow of the doorway and looked up sharply and Jevan, quickly, followed her glance.

The patch became Marcus Pett's handsome waistcoat. He came forward into the pool of light from the table lamp.

"May I come in?" he said jauntily after he was already in. "Cary's resting. God, what a day! Is the paper there? May I see it? Jevan, my boy, I could do with a highball. There's a little business I'd like to talk to you about."

CHAPTER 10

IT WAS SOPHIE who came to the rescue and guided Marcus away and downstairs. He went without much reluctance.

"It's about my trustee's report," he said to Jevan. "Everything's ready. I'll turn the papers over to you any time. Tomorrow? Very well. It's all ready. Your wife is a rich young woman, Jevan. But of course you know that. Yes, yes, Sophie. I'm coming. Wait till I kiss the bride. I didn't get a chance to downstairs with all the people buzzing around."

He kissed Dorcas with a flourish and went away, propelled suavely by Sophie.

Afterward Dorcas remembered her wedding dinner; served at the little table drawn up before the fire with its glow upon the lace and glimmering in the crystal and silver, with candlelight on the table and a low vase of red roses and Jevan's eyes unfathomable beyond the glow of the candles.

Afterward, too, she remembered that they talked, in circles, of the murder. The detective did not telephone and did not come. About ten, however, there was a telephone call for Jevan. He returned from it looking pleased. "It was Willy," he said but did not explain. "My bags have come; Bench put them in my room. Here's something I want you to take."

He had a glass of water and a capsule. "It's a sedative. I got it from Cary."

"But I——"

"Take it."

She took it, choking a little on the capsule. He stood a moment looking down at her. "That's good," he said, then abruptly, "Good night, Dorcas."

He went away abruptly, too, closing the door firmly, and did not return.

All night long the wind and sleet continued intermittently. Now and then Dorcas roused to hear sleet beating gustily at the black windows. Morning was still cold and dark. Mamie brought her breakfast tray and a wool jacket.

"It's bitter cold out, Miss Dorcas."

"Are the morning papers here?"

"Mr Jevan has them." Mamie smiled. "It's good to have a man in the house, Miss Dorcas. We would have called the police this morning when Bench found it but I thought of Mr Jevan and he was informed and said not to call the police."

"When Bench found what?" said Dorcas, sitting up abruptly. The dishes on the tray clattered and Mamie grasped and steadied it swiftly.

"That the house was entered last night, of course. I thought Mr Jevan had told you." She gave Dorcas a curious, swiftly withdrawn glance and went to close the windows.

"The house entered! What on earth do you mean, Mamie? A burglar?"

Mamie's neatly striped blue shoulders lifted.

"Nobody knows. Nothing was taken. It was the little door in the back—the grade door beside the basement steps. Standing wide open this morning, it was. Wind and sleet blowing in and the whole house open to any tramp going by. It's just a lucky thing we weren't all murdered in our beds."

"What did Mr Jevan do?" inquired Dorcas slowly.

Again the woman gave her a veiled, swiftly withdrawn glance. She replied: "He came right away and looked and said not to call the police. Nothing was missing that we could discover. There were some smudges of dirt on the floor that might have been footprints but nothing else."

"Where is Mr Jevan now?"

"Having his breakfast, miss. Shall I——"

"No, no," said Dorcas quickly. "That's all, Mamie. Thank you."

So began Friday, March thirteenth—a dark, stormy day with lights on all over the great gloomy house. With newspapers and telephone calls and the doctor coming to see

Cary. With caterers' men removing chairs and ferns; with servants cleaning and rearranging the vast, chilly rooms downstairs. With roses all over the house left over from the wedding and fully opened so their fragrance drifted along the halls. With Marcus Pett arriving shortly before lunch.

The telephone calls that day were the worst, although the newspapers were even then, subtly, beginning to change. One of the newspapers carried along with the story of Ronald's murder and on the front page a paragraph stating that Mr and Mrs Jevan Locke, whose marriage had taken place the day following the murder, had not yet gone on their wedding trip; it observed without further conjecture that they had been questioned by the police.

That was one of the more conservative newspapers. Dorcas did not see the *Call*.

But others did and went to telephones.

WHIPPLE HEIRESS HELD IN MURDER INQUIRY. The headline from the paper repeated itself endlessly over telephone wires, and eventually, a little cautiously, friends began to telephone to the Whipple house. Cary's friends mostly, and loyally, yet with inquiries that were beginning to be a little edged with something more—or less—than friendly anxiety. However, that day the main note struck was indignation. WHIPPLE HEIRESS HELD IN MURDER INQUIRY: it was preposterous, outrageous. Yet—had the police really refused to permit Dorcas and Jevan to go on their wedding trip? And if so, why?

Sophie took most of the telephone calls, coming away with a wry face and giving very brief messages to Cary. "Mrs Mortimer telephoned," she would say. And that was all. After the first few times Cary did not question further.

Jevan might have been a hundred miles away for all Dorcas saw of him that morning. He did not come to her room; she heard nothing of or from him until about eleven, when Marcus arrived.

They were waiting, Mamie told her, in her father's study. Dorcas roused from staring out at the leaden sky and thinking in deep, troubled circles, dressed in one of her trousseau gowns, a soft, leaf-green wool, and went down. Her mother's door was closed; Sophie was nowhere to be seen. In the drawing room men in gray aprons were carrying out pots of ferns. She went along the narrow hall and, again, entered her father's study. Marcus bobbed up quickly from his chair.

"Good morning, my dear. Good morning." Jevan rose and said nothing.

Somebody pushed forward a chair for her. On the table was a leather brief case, packed and bulging. Marcus said: "It's right that you should be present, my dear. I'm turning over your affairs to your husband. From now on you are his responsibility, not mine. Ha, ha. Well, now, here we are. Here we are."

He looked old and tired in the cruelly clear light above his head. The pouches under his eyes were heavy; his hands trembled a little as he fumbled among the papers.

"Your wife is a very rich woman, Jevan," he went on. "Here are the reports of all transactions I have made in her name. Here is my power of attorney—no, that's a list of securities. Well, anyway, it's here somewhere." He dropped the papers, fumbled in an inner pocket for thick eyeglasses and adjusted them.

Jevan looked quietly at Dorcas. "We had an uninvited caller last night."

"Mamie told me."

"Apparently nothing was taken. There was no point in calling the police."

"Police," said Marcus. "What's all this? Do you mean the house was entered?"

"Only that, apparently. A little door in the back was found open this morning. It's very rarely used. Nobody could remember when it was last used. Nothing was taken, however."

"Good God," cried Marcus, his eyes bulging. "Good heavens! Why should anyone enter the house and not take anything? I mean—good heavens, Jevan, you should get the police."

"Why?"

"Why! Because that's what the police are for. Protection. Good God——"

"But, Marcus, nothing was stolen. What complaint would we have? Besides, I didn't want to call the police."

"But the thing is so pointless, so——"

"That's it," said Jevan. "No point to it. The door is now closed and locked and we searched the place and found no one." He smiled a little ruefully. "Searching this house is no small job. The cellars alone—I didn't know it was such an enormous house, Dorcas. There are fruit cellars and wine cellars and storage rooms and coal cellars. The laundry chutes alone are big enough for elevators—or nearly. Your father certainly had his notions of comfort. Or ideas about families; you ought to have had a dozen or so brothers and sisters. Even then the house would be too big. Ever been on the third floor, Marcus?"

Marcus shook his head. He looked a little bored and, under the harsh light, gray and lined as if overnight the thin, cobwebby film of old age had fastened itself upon him. Jevan went on cheerfully:

"Besides the servants' rooms there's a couple of game rooms; furniture all sheeted; a piano in one room; a billiard table so big it will have to stay here until the house dissolves, for it could never be moved. Well, anyway, we searched the place and I hope to God we never have to live here, Dorcas, I thought I was doing fairly well for a rising young broker but I can't keep up a place like this."

"You won't need to," Marcus pointed out. "There's all Dorcas' money——"

"No, thank you," said Jevan politely. "I support my wife. At least I supply her food and her roof. If she finds sable coats and star sapphires necessary to her existence she can go and buy them with her own money. But she eats my food and lives under a roof I can supply."

"But, my dear boy!" Marcus was plainly aghast. "Here's all this money. What are you going to do with it?"

"Turn it straight back to you. Form another trusteeship. Unless Dorcas wants to manage it herself."

"Turn it——" Marcus dropped the papers in his hand and leaned back in his chair. His eyes bulged and his mouth opened. "Do you mean that, Jevan?"

"Certainly."

"But Dorcas——"

"Dorcas has nothing to do with it."

"But—but it's her money."

"She's my wife. Unless she wants to manage the money herself. Do you, Dorcas?" he said directly.

"Yes," said Dorcas. "No."

"Huh," said Marcus in a disorganized way.

Jevan smiled. "She means, I imagine, that she would have to learn. I can help her if she wants me to. But I'll not take charge of her money and I'll not use it and so far as I'm concerned you can simply take your papers back. Dorcas can go through them some day at her leisure. But in the meantime you'd better carry on. Right, Dorcas?"

"Yes, I suppose so," said Dorcas a little reluctantly and Marcus jerked abruptly toward Jevan.

"Carry on!" he cried sharply. "What do you mean?"

"It's this business of Drew's murder——"

"Unfortunate," said Marcus, fingering his mustache. "Most unfortunate."

"Well," said Jevan dubiously. "I suppose you can call it that. At any rate you knew the police were here yesterday."

"Yes." He sat down.

"They are likely to come again. There's no evidence, of course, that leads them to think either Dorcas or I had any— knew anything of the murder. There's no reason, except the fact that we both knew him, to lead them to think that we can inform them of anything in his life or circumstances that would lead to the murderer." He said it all coolly, very clearly, very definitely, and waited an instant for it to sink into Marcus' troubled perceptions. "But nevertheless I think they'll be back to question some more. It may be that for— oh, some time (until they find the murderer or get some line on him) we'll be sort of preoccupied with the affair. I hope not. As soon as they let us, however, we'll take our honeymoon trip. When we return Dorcas will examine all these reports. I'll help her if she wants me to. But until then I think you'd better go on as usual. If you will. Does that suit you, Dorcas?"

"Yes. Yes, perfectly. Will you, Marcus?"

"Why, of course. Certainly. By all means. My poor dear child, I know exactly how you feel." He looked at the reports and apparently was aware of the faint trembling of his hands, like a beginning palsy, for he put them down tight upon the bundles of papers. "Certainly," he repeated briskly. "But don't thank me. Don't thank me. I'm only too glad to do anything I can for you. And as a matter of fact it's a very good arrangement. You can't take things over in ten minutes time and the markets just now are very jumpy. Very jumpy," said Marcus, thoughtful for an instant, with gray cobwebs over his face again. But he rose energetically. "Shall I take the reports with me, Jevan? Yes, I think I'd better just take them along."

"It doesn't matter," said Jevan rather quickly. "There's a safe here somewhere, I expect."

"Back of the picture," said Dorcas and told them how to slide the stag aside and, when the safe was disclosed, how to open it.

"Somewhat antiquated," said Marcus doubtfully. "Are you sure you don't want me to take them to my office safe?"

Jevan frowned. "There's nothing here a burglar might want, is there, Marcus?"

"No. No, certainly not."

"They'll be all right here then," said Jevan and put the reports and the brief case in the safe. Marcus watched him a little dubiously but went away briskly enough, bowing gallantly over Dorcas' hand and striding down the corridor with the step and carriage of a younger man. And he must have met the detective on the step, for he had barely gone, and Jevan had turned to Dorcas briskly and begun to say something about the trusteeship and Marcus, when Bench came to the study door. He looked pale and very distressed and said the man was there again.

"Who?"

"The police, sir. That is, the—the detective. The one that was here yesterday."

He didn't mention the two detectives who had accompanied Jacob Wait and neither Dorcas nor Jevan thought of them either, but thought instead and immediately of Wait.

"Oh," said Jevan. "Wait." He glanced at Dorcas. "Send him in."

Dorcas was standing, her heart pounding furiously, her breath jerky. She clutched at the back of the chair near her with stiff, frightened fingers.

Jevan was standing, too, lighting another cigarette. Bench hesitated and said: "There's a man with him. Not a policeman. Shall I permit him——"

"Certainly. All of them."

"Yes sir."

"Jevan—I didn't expect them so soon. What shall I——"

"I didn't either. I thought there'd be time to talk. But there'd be nothing more to say. I mean, you're to deny having been there. Deny everything. Believe me, it's the only way to do; trust me, Dorcas."

He said it suddenly, pleadingly. He took a long step nearer

her and looked down into her eyes and said again: "Trust me—my wife."

Dorcas did not speak. She was suddenly very much afraid of a little, sallow-faced man who walked like a cat and had somber dark eyes, and what Jevan said scarcely reached her. But he turned abruptly away and added in his usual, pleasantly impersonal way: "Take it easy, Dorcas. Try not to look so guilty."

Bench came to the door and stood aside and Jacob Wait appeared in the doorway. His black, glossy hair made his features pale by contrast, looming out of the dimly lighted hall. He wore a heavy brown burberry; perhaps Bench had made no offer to take it from him. He looked at Dorcas and at Jevan and turned to someone following him.

"In here," he said in an unexpectedly full, rich voice and entered the room. The man following him entered too. He was tall and extremely well built and did not wear a uniform but, instead, rather shabby dark clothing. He glanced at Jevan and very quickly away, as if he did not want to meet Jevan's eyes. He looked fully and boldly at Dorcas, however, and Wait amazingly took a hundred-dollar bill from his pocket and laid it on the table. Jevan started to say something and stopped. Wait's small, graceful hand lingered upon the bill and he said: "Well, how about it?"

The man replied at once. "That's the woman," he said. "That's the woman who was with Drew the night he was killed. I'd know her anywhere."

CHAPTER 11

IT WAS, it must be, the doorman.

Dorcas sought for something memorable about him, something recognizable, but there was nothing. Jevan said: "Who is this? What do you mean by bringing this man here?"

"His name is McFee. He is the doorman for the apartment house where Ronald Drew lived. He saw Miss Whipple arrive with Drew and enter the apartment house a short time before Drew was murdered."

"The man is mistaken," said Jevan shortly. "He saw some-one else. You can ask anyone in the house, Wait; they'll tell you Mrs Locke was here. She has a perfect alibi."

"Oh, *has* she," said Wait. "Well, that's fine. But she couldn't be in two places at once. Therefore I am obliged to arrest——"

"What's that hundred-dollar bill for?"

Wait smiled. "Doormen don't customarily go about trying to change hundred-dollar bills. It's routine; he was being watched and he tried to get change for it; in five minutes he admitted that he'd had a typewritten note enclosing the bill and telling him not to identify a woman he would be asked to identify."

"So you think I gave it to him. You are wrong, Wait. Look at me, McFee." McFee looked once in deep embarrassment and quickly away. "No, look at *me*. Now then, did you ever see me before?"

"No," said McFee, not looking. "No sir."

"Sure about that?" said Wait. "Remember the man who went up to Drew's apartment later on. Are you sure this wasn't the man?"

McFee's Adam's apple went up and down and he stared at the stag, who returned his gaze remotely.

"No, Mr Wait."

"What's that! Did you see this man? Can you identify him? Look at him."

McFee wouldn't. He gave one scared look at Wait and sought the stag again swiftly. "I meant, no sir, Mr Wait. I meant, I don't know. I only saw the man enter the elevator. Just his back—a dark overcoat, a felt hat. I wouldn't know him again. I didn't see him leave. I'm new in the building and don't know all the regulars yet. He might have been anybody. I——"

Wait stopped him. Jevan was smiling. Wait said quickly: "That'll do, McFee."

"There goes your witness," said Jevan.

"He identified Mrs Locke," said Wait. "Now then, Mrs Locke, when you went to Drew's apartment with——"

Sophie opened the door and entered. Sophie, dressed for the street in a green tweed suit with the long coat fastened over a skirt which was undoubtedly much too tight.

"Dorcas," she said, saw the two men and stopped too abruptly. McFee, clutched by the little silence, tore his eyes from the stag, saw Sophie, saw the green suit, let his jaw fall in a look of consternation and said: "Oh——"

"What is it, McFee?" cried Jevan quickly. "Is that the woman you saw?"

"Yes," said McFee. "No. I don't know. I——"

"Stop that," snapped Wait. "Shut up, you fool, you. You've already identified the woman——"

"Not much of an identification, Wait," said Jevan. "No. You're wrong. He's admitted before three people that he doesn't know. That identification is no good. All he remembers is a green suit. Any woman in a green suit would look like that woman you saw. Isn't that right, McFee?"

The doorman was angry. He had flushed a deep crimson and was fumbling for his hat.

"I'm going," he said. "You can't keep me here, making a fool of me. I'm going and I won't say another word."

"But you don't know which woman it was that you saw? Isn't that right, McFee? Look at them both. Look at them. Now can you swear that it was one or the other?" Dorcas was as still as a doll; she felt as if her very face were wax and had the truth written over it. Sophie, collectedly, swayed a little so McFee saw her profile with the little hat pulled low and the big fur collar pulled high. McFee, angry, looked at her and then at Dorcas and back to Sophie.

"See, you don't know! You can't tell! It might be either of them. It might be a hundred other women. You can't go into a court and swear a woman's life away on an identification like that. You——"

McFee muttered something, gave a bitter glance at the hundred-dollar bill and started for the door.

"I'm going," he said. "You're making a fool of me. I'm going——"

"Nobody can make a fool of you," said Jacob Wait neatly. "Keep your hundred dollars, Locke."

He pushed the bill toward Jevan, who made no move to take it, and Wait, having no use apparently for the small amenity of leave-taking, vanished instantly in the wake of an already sullenly vanished McFee.

Sophie reached under her coat and unfastened her tight skirt and sighed.

"How much do you weigh, Dorcas?" she said. "I can't take a deep breath with this skirt fastened!"

"Sophie, you shouldn't have done it."

"Why not? It worked, didn't it? And I wasn't in any danger, for I wasn't at the apartment house and nobody could possibly prove that I was."

"You did it in the very nick of time, Sophie." Jevan picked up the hundred-dollar bill, smoothed it in his fingers and laughed shortly. "Like Willy, wasn't it, to give it to him in a hundred-dollar bill. Why couldn't he have made it tens?"

"Willy——"

He gave Dorcas an impatient look. "I phoned Willy last night after you told me the doorman actually saw you. Told him to fix the doorman. Told him to write a note on some public typewriter, enclose the money and get it to the fellow. So he did. Except that I didn't tell him to make it small bills and he just simply put in a hundred-dollar bill."

"Then Willy knows too," said Sophie.

"Yes," said Jevan. "Well, there's nothing we can do. If I only knew why he is concentrating on you, Dorcas. Is there anything that you haven't told me? Any scrap of evidence, no matter how small?"

There wasn't. In the end they were obliged to leave the thing unsolved. And there was nothing they could do.

The day wore on. There were more telephone calls. Servants finished clearing the house, and restored the spacious rooms to their usual shining, somber order.

Late in the afternoon Dorcas went to Cary's room and found her pale and worried with her lovely blue eyes rimmed in pink.

"If the police would only let you go on your wedding trip," she said. "I know that everybody's talking about it."

Cary, of course, didn't know and mustn't know why the police would not let her leave. Dorcas answered evasively and presently went away.

Late in the afternoon, too, Willy Devany came. Came with elaborate circumspection so there was actually something like stealth in the way he slid in the front door, startling Bench.

"The police," he said breathlessly. "I'm followed. I've been grilled, Bench. Grilled."

"Your hat, sir."

"Grilled," repeated Willy a trifle wildly and asked for Jevan.

Their conversation, however, was lengthy and private, with the study door closed.

Dorcas wandered about the house, listening for their emerging, going from one gray window to another, thinking in circles that had no beginning and no end.

Yesterday at about this time the wedding guests were beginning to leave. Her wedding seemed as unreal as everything else in that suddenly topsy-turvy world. Unreal and at the same time paradoxically and poignantly real.

For Jevan was there in the house, in the study which seemed to become his own. How immediately the household had adopted him; how immediately and automatically he had become the head of the house! "It's good," Mamie had said, "to have a man in the house." Her husband. And what did she know of him? What did she know of this marriage she had made except that already she knew that it was not the thing she had expected it to be! For it was different; the calm, smooth, untroubled sea she had expected her marriage to Jevan to float quietly upon was full of hidden, unplumbed depths and sweeping currents. And Jevan himself, mysteriously, was different.

What had Jevan found when he came to Ronald's apartment? Why had he come? What could have happened between the time of her own hurried departure from that mirror-lined apartment, with its dead white and dull blue shadows, and Jevan's arrival? Or had it happened after Jevan's arrival? Had Jevan killed Ronald?

It was not the first or the last time the thing forced its way into her conscious mind: could Jevan have done this thing? Jevan, who had, besides basic common sense, so strong a strain of ruthlessness. Jevan, who hated Ronald and made no bones of it. Jevan, who had had opportunity.

But if Jevan had killed Ronald he must have had a motive and his motive could not be jealousy.

And he had said with an effect of truth that he had not killed Ronald. He had said it impatiently, as if, if he had murdered Ronald, he would not have hesitated to admit it. To her at least. His wife. His wife—and yet, in this strangely perplexing, suddenly important thing called marriage, not his wife.

Willy was leaving. She heard his voice and Jevan's in the hall and growing nearer; then Jevan said: "All right, Willy." And Willy said: "See you later," and came along the hall toward the outside door. As he passed the drawing-room door he looked in and saw her, hesitated and came in.

"Hello, Dorcas."

He was a little pale and excited and breathless. His thin blond hair was ruffled and his blue eyes sought her own anxiously.

He came closer to her and peered at her worriedly.

"Now look here, Dorcas. You mustn't be so—so upset about all this. Brooding around in the dark. Why don't you turn on some lights?" He peered closer, took one of her hands in his own and patted it.

"You're not—not grieving over Ronald, are you?" he said as if struck by the thought suddenly. "He's not worth grieving over. You—why, Dorcas, I never dreamed you really—cared about him."

"I didn't—that is, I don't."

For a moment he looked deeply into her eyes as if to be sure she had told him the truth. Then he sighed as if with relief.

"Thank God you weren't in love with Ronald. He—oh, there's no use going into the reasons. But—gosh, Dorcas, if you had been in love with him and——"

"And?"

"Nothing," said Willy. "That is, I was only thinking how tough it would be for you. Of course it's bad enough as it is, but if you'd been in love with him——" He stopped again and looked at her and said unexpectedly: "Listen, dear, if there's anything troubling you that—I mean if there's anything I can do for you, you'll tell me, won't you? You see," said Willy simply, "I love you. Too."

He meant it. There was no possible doubt of that. He put her hand a little awkwardly to his cheek and looked at her with lighted, purposeful blue eyes and repeated it: "I love you, Dorcas. I've always loved you. Since we were kids. Oh, I've never had the nerve to tell you; you never needed me before . . ." He faltered there and then said: "Before this. I knew you didn't love me."

"I'm—sorry. . . ."

"Oh, it's all right, Dorcas. You're in love with Jevan and you'll be happy."

"But——" She checked the denial on her lips and Willy went on: "Jevan knows I love you. He's always known it. That's why," said Willy rather wistfully, "he's so good to me."

"Oh, my dear," cried Dorcas. "Don't! Jevan is your friend. As I am, Willy."

"I know you're fond of me. I only told you all this because I wanted you to know that I would do anything in the world for you. Anything," repeated Willy with the deep, fervent flame of a zealot burning in his blue eyes.

"Willy, I—I can't tell you what——"

"Don't try," said Willy cheerfully. "I only want you to know you can depend upon me. With my life," said Willy calmly. "Hello—what's that?"

Dorcas heard it too. Someone being let into the hall and speaking to Bench and the door being closed.

"Is Mr Devany here?"

"Yes sir." That was Bench.

"It's Wait," said Willy. "Again. He's been after me twice; you'd think I shot Ronald. . . . All right, Bench," he said in a louder voice, going to the door. "I'm in here. Hello, Wait."

Dorcas turned on lights as Wait entered the room. He blinked.

"Don't go, Mrs Locke," he said quickly as Dorcas moved toward the door. "I only want to talk to Devany a moment or two."

Dorcas sank into a chair and Willy looked at Wait and said irritably: "All right. Shoot. What is it?"

"What car were you driving Wednesday night when you say you picked up Locke at the club and took him home?"

"What car?" Willy's light eyebrows lifted. "Why, I think the Cadillac sedan. Why?"

"Tell me again exactly what you did, say, from seven o'clock on."

"Oh, all right," said Willy. "At seven o'clock I was home. At seven-thirty—no, perhaps a little earlier, I had dinner. Ask my servants and——"

"I have. Go on. You had finished dinner by a quarter to eight."

"Yes. Then I had the car brought round and dismissed the chauffeur."

"Right. At ten minutes to eight, your chauffeur says: he got to the eight o'clock movie over on Sixty-third."

"Did he? Well—well, then I just drove around a little."

"Where?"

"I don't know—oh yes, I went through the Midway, I think, and then I went to see Jevan."

"What time exactly did you reach the Locke place?"

Willy said, blue eyes rather narrow, that he didn't know. "Jevan wasn't there. He is closing the old place, intending to sell it; nobody was there but the cook and a maid. They didn't know where he was——"

"The maid who answered the door said it was about a quarter to nine when you came."

"Did she? Well, perhaps it was. Naturally I didn't notice particularly."

"Then you had no appointment with Locke?"

"No. That is, I just—wanted to see him. Had nothing else to do. Was to be his best man, you know, next day, so I——" Willy's eyes brightened and he said quickly: "I wanted to be sure everything was set. That's all."

"So you went to the Locke house. You reached the house at a quarter to nine, having left your own house at ten minutes to eight. That's quite a gap in time. Were you here at this house in the interval?"

"You mean *here*? At this house? Why, no. Certainly not," said Willy sweepingly.

"How about that, Mrs Locke?" Wait turned quickly to Dorcas.

"No, Willy wasn't here," she said hurriedly. And remembered the long car which had passed so slowly during the moment she had met Ronald, spoken to him, permitted him —so foolishly and mistakenly—to lead her to the taxi he had waiting. Could it have been Willy driving the car? But if it had been it meant nothing. Only that he might have seen them together.

"A Cadillac sedan," said Wait thoughtfully. "Did you drive to Drew's apartment, Devany?"

"Why would I go there? Certainly not."

"That's interesting," said Wait. "You see, a Cadillac sedan drew up and stopped just behind the taxi in which Drew and his woman companion arrived at the apartment house Wednesday night. The doorman went from Drew's taxi to open the door for the driver of the sedan, who, however, did not get out of the car just then. The doorman waited and then heard the telephone ring and had to go inside. The car had gone when he returned."

"I don't know what you're talking about, Wait. I can't be held responsible for every Cadillac sedan in the city."

"I think," said Wait, "that this was your car. And I think it was your Cadillac sedan that later on, according to the doorman, was parked across the street from the apartment building for at least half an hour—between nine-thirty and ten. Was it?"

"Ah," said Willy pleasantly. "That's the time for which I have an alibi. I picked up Locke at the club at nine-thirty and was with him from then on till about eleven."

"Drew," said Wait, "could have been murdered any time after eight-fifteen when the doorman saw him alive. . . . Why were you following Drew?"

"I was not," said Willy flatly, with his pointed, delicate chin up.

"Who was the woman with him?"

"I don't—I tell you I wasn't there."

"You're lying," said Wait and, as appeared to be his customary manner of departure, went away without another word.

"Gosh," said Willy and touched his forehead with a handkerchief. "Gosh. . . . Well, there's no talk of license numbers. Good night, Dorcas." He went away as abruptly as Wait had done.

And Dorcas sat in the twilight, staring at the glow of light from the lamp upon an old rug, and not seeing it. Willy—but Willy wouldn't kill a mouse. And Jevan, who had force that Willy lacked, had actually been in Ronald's apartment and coolly admitted it.

Dinner that night was served, without orders to that effect, in the big dining room. It was another note of recognition to Jevan's presence. A man in the house, occupying a high-backed armchair at the head of the table.

Dorcas wore one of her trousseau gowns, a misty gray chiffon, as lovely as a foggy sea. She wore an emerald at her throat and her hair shone gold in the mellow glow from candles. But if Jevan had eyes for the gown—or for her—she did not perceive it. He talked coolly and abstractedly to Sophie about European travel and war in Spain.

Later over coffee in the long library she looked at him and thought of dancing around that library only twenty-four hours ago, dancing over bare and polished floors in her white satin with his arm tight around her, holding her to him.

Now Jevan was remote, impersonal, looking at magazines, getting a foreign news bulletin on the radio and commenting upon it. About eleven Bench came into the room, spoke to Jevan quietly and he rose, said something vague and followed Bench out of the room.

Sophie, hazel eyes curious, got up presently and went away, her suavely fitted, flesh-colored lace trailing gracefully behind her. She came back almost at once with a newspaper under her arm.

"He's seeing to the locks—windows, doors, everywhere. The paper was in the butler's pantry." She opened it across a table and Dorcas came to stand beside her.

There were several columns. The headlines shouted murder and Ronald Drew. At the end of the second column Dorcas' name appeared.

"It's his telephone call to you," said Sophie and pointed with her unexpectedly blunt forefinger.

Perhaps after a while I shall get hardened to it, thought Dorcas, aware again of that sickening wince inside her as she saw her own name.

The murdered man had put in a telephone call to Mrs Locke a short time before his murder. Up to the time of the announcement of Mrs Locke's engagement to Jevan Locke (young broker and son of the late Jevan A. Locke, of the Stock Exchange) she had been seen frequently in the company of Ronald Drew and there was an apparently well-authenticated rumor that she and Drew were to marry.

Cringing and hating herself for cringing, Dorcas read on.

The Whipple family; the Lockes; Drew's death at first supposed a suicide due to despondency; inquiry in the hands of Jacob Wait, new to the city staff (here followed a brief but pungent account of Wait's activities in Wrexe County); and Mr and Mrs Locke had not yet gone on their wedding trip but were being detained for questioning.

"It could be worse," said Sophie. "But we'd better not let your mother see the papers. . . . I'm going to bed."

Dorcas followed, thinking in spite of herself of the white divan in Ronald's apartment, the look on his face as he had flung the telephone to the floor, the way the taxi driver had scrutinized her when she hailed him. *The taxi driver!*

She'd forgotten him.

Her hands, busy with the fastenings of the gray chiffon, were suddenly cold and clumsy. She was becoming acquainted, she thought fantastically, with fear. But the taxi driver wouldn't remember her. How could he? So many fares, so many faces, so many addresses.

It was close to midnight when Jevan knocked at the door leading into his room and, as she replied, came in. He wore a brown dressing gown over his pajamas and went to the door which led into the hall.

"Does this lock?"

She put aside the book she had been trying to read and sat up. "I don't know. Why?"

"No reason," said Jevan and found an old-fashioned bolt let into the casing and turned it. "You all right, Dorcas?" he said then, glancing at her.

"Quite."

"That's good," said Jevan coolly. "Good night." The door closed again behind him and after a long time Dorcas picked up her book. But she couldn't read and presently she put out the lamp beside her. She wished he hadn't thought it was necessary to lock the door. And she wondered what he was thinking of in the silence and darkness of the room adjoining her own.

Outside the night darkened. Shrubbery huddled closer in the corners of the gaunt fence. Gradually the few remaining lights in the house vanished. In the hall the bronze boy still held a faint, amber light which left the corners and the open doors leading to other rooms crowded and suffused with deep, cavernous shadows.

It must have been about three o'clock when Dorcas roused to hear the telephone ringing, faint and distant and imperious in the silent black depths of the house.

CHAPTER 12

SHE WENT, at last, to answer it.

Slipping quietly out of bed, thrusting bare, small feet into flat slippers, fur lined and heelless, wrapping a long, warm negligee around her. She opened the door, and because that sharp summons was so singularly imperative, because, perhaps, she was not fully awake and did not think of her own telephone that was nearer—or perhaps because fate stepped in and demanded the making of that one small, tremendously important link in the darkly patterned chain—because of all this or because of nothing she went downstairs, thinking urgently and only of the main telephone off the hall below.

Her feet made no sound on the carpeted steps, her hand slid quietly along the polished railing. As she reached the area of light cast by the torch in the bronze boy's hand she stopped, momentarily daunted by the blackness of the cavernous openings of other rooms from the hall below her.

The telephone rang again and she ran down the remaining stairs and into the darkness leading off at her right.

It was the narrow side passageway which led past the telephone closet, an entrance to the laundry chute and thence to Penn Whipple's study. At the end of the passage, lost completely now in darkness, was the side entrance which emerged onto the porte-cochère.

She groped for the handle of the telephone door, found and opened it. Or thought she opened it. Instead a cold, dampish current of air struck her face and with it the unmistakable, musty odor of cellars. She pulled back abruptly. It was the laundry chute of course; she closed the door and it clicked sharply into place. The telephone pealed again and she groped along the wall. She found the door to the telephone closet, went in and automatically closed it behind her.

But when she grasped the telephone and answered no one replied. She spoke again and again and finally, fumblingly in the darkness, replaced the telephone. It was some mistake of course. She opened the door. And opened it upon a completely dark hall with no light leading from the bronze boy. No light anywhere. She caught her breath sharply with surprise and stopped.

And it was just then that the thing occurred that, then, had no meaning and no explanation but always to Dorcas had the very essence of reality.

For she heard it clearly, altogether unmistakable in the stillness, and that was the small, neat click of the door of the laundry chute.

Just that.

That and the fact that the bronze boy's small light no longer burned and nothing more.

She was all at once, chokingly, every pulse leaping, frightened. She ran. Through the darkness and up the stairs.

A faint stream of light came from the guest-room wing and she ran stumblingly into it and into Jevan's arms.

The light was coming from the door to his room which was open. He grasped her tightly in his arms, so her heart thudded frantically against him.

"Dorcas, what is it? Where have you been? What——"

"Downstairs." Her voice was muffled against his heart so he had to bend his head to hear her. "There's something—somebody——"

"I can't understand, Dorcas. Tell me——" He drew her into his room and closed the door and sat down, holding her cradled in his arms. "Now tell me. Don't be frightened."

There was so little to tell. Yet when he heard he rose and put her down in the chair and went to a table. Light flashed on a revolver and Dorcas cried: "No—no—don't——"

"I won't be long. If there's nobody there it's all right. If there's somebody down there I want to know."

"Don't——"

But he had gone.

It seemed a long time before he returned, gave her a quick look, closed the door and thoughtfully put the revolver down on the table.

"What did you find? Who——"

"Nobody," he said. "And nothing—except the light in the bronze boy was turned out. Not burned out. And the door, the little grade door at the back of the house that was opened last night, was standing open again."

"But you had locked it."

"Yes. I locked it myself. But somebody could have entered the basement somehow and got into the house by way of the laundry chute. He could easily have escaped, then, by the grade door. Unless he had some way of burgling the lock he must have opened the grade door from the inside; it certainly isn't very likely that anyone would have the key to that door. Although its having been opened twice seems to indicate tonight's prowler and last night's are the same. At any rate the grade door certainly could provide an exit. The light in the hall had been turned out while you were at the telephone."

"Then someone was in the hall——"

"He could have been. Or he could have heard your voice

and taken refuge in the chute and escaped by the grade door as soon as you were gone. The laundry chute is plenty big enough for anybody to get into. And thus have access to the whole house."

Her skin prickled.

"Oh no, Jevan. It isn't possible."

"It's quite possible. There's a kind of rough ladder—pieces of board nailed to studding—I looked. Must have been there forever. But whoever used it would have to know something of the house."

"No one was there. I feel sure. A draft from somewhere forced the door shut and I happened to hear it."

"And the bronze boy got down from the newel post and walked over and turned himself out at the switch and went back to the newel post."

She didn't answer. He said, watching her: "We can't do anything tonight. I closed and locked the grade door. It has no bolt but I'll have one put on it tomorrow. It'll be a Houdini," said Jevan, looking very grim, "that gets in this house tomorrow night. Come, Dorcas. You're going back to bed."

He led her back through the little dressing room to her own room. Saw that she got into bed and pulled the eiderdown to her chin.

"You're still scared," he said, looking down at her. "It's no wonder. Do you . . ." He hesitated and said: "Shall I leave the door open so you can call to me if anything—if you want me?"

"Yes," she said in a small voice. His look deepened, and he smiled.

"You look like a scared little kid. Your eyes are so big and bright." He put out one hand abruptly and pushed her hair back from her face and unexpectedly sat down beside her. The amused, half-tender little smile vanished and he took her in his arms closely, brusquely, his mouth all at once upon her own.

"Dorcas," he said, whispering, and kissed her again.

Then quietly, with queerly gentle abruptness, he put her back and rose. Still quietly and rather deliberately he crossed the room.

For a few moments she could hear him moving about in his own room, then the light went off. After a long time she turned off the light upon the little table beside her.

CHAPTER 13

IN THE MORNING they talked it over, Dorcas and Jevan, distantly, politely, with no faint recognition, unless it was in that very politeness, of a moment the night had also brought.

He had, he told her, discovered nothing more of their nocturnal visitor.

"But I don't like these entrances and escapes by night and I'm going to stop them," he said. Again by common consent they did not tell Cary.

Sophie came upon Bench and Jevan in the back entry, driving nails into the casing of the small grade door and building an impromptu but solid wooden bolt across it. And even Sophie, whose poise was not readily shaken, looked upset when they told her the house had been entered again.

"Why?"

"I don't know." Jevan took some nails out of his mouth and stood up, regarding his work with a critical eye.

"But—but there's nothing in the house," said Sophie. "Cary's jewels are kept in safe deposit; there's simply nothing to warrant a burglary. Unless they are after the flat silver! Or perhaps it's the Rembrandt Penn bought just before he died and they don't know it's not a Rembrandt." ·

"Perhaps. Give me the hammer, Bench."

Sophie was staring at the nails, her hazel eyes dark and somber.

"It's not very pleasant, is it?" she said suddenly. "Somebody entering and wandering about this old place at night. After Ronald's murder. . . . After all, there is such a thing as a homicidal maniac."

"Sophie!" cried Dorcas sharply. "Don't!"

Bench sighed and drove another nail morosely and the doorbell rang.

It was a detective. He was shown into the drawing room and he asked for Jevan and for Dorcas and told them briefly that he wasn't satisfied with Jevan's story of his own activities on the night of the murder.

Jevan did not seem perturbed.

"Did you inquire about what you call my activities at the club?"

"Certainly," said Wait, allowing his attention to be caught and immediately relinquished by the spurious Rembrandt on the opposite wall.

"And didn't you find several men who saw and spoke to me?"

"By all means. None of whom knew exactly what time he had seen you. And all of whom were very much more interested in knowing why I was making the inquiry than in anything else. Oh, I'll grant you," acknowledged Wait with a small wave of his hand, "there were several efforts in your behalf. Did you have a scotch and soda at the club bar with one Tom Wilkins at ten o'clock?"

"Good old Tom."

"Exactly. Devany says you were with him in his car at ten."

"That's right."

"Did you and Devany make any stops between the club and your house?"

"You mean, I suppose, did we go to Drew's apartment and kill him?"

"Drew was murdered," said Wait incontrovertibly. He added simply and with the weight that plain, direct truth always carries: "Where there is murder there is motive. In a man's life there are not many people who stand in so close and strong a relationship to him that a motive for murder exists between them. . . . The night Drew was murdered a woman came to his apartment. A man, probably, came later. I must find that woman and that man."

There was a small silence. Jevan and the detective looked steadily at each other. Dorcas sat perfectly still. Away off somewhere in the house a door closed and someone—Sophie or Cary or one of the maids—passed quietly along the hall. Jevan said at last, gravely:

"Look here, Wait. Neither my wife nor I want to go through life under suspicion of having done murder We are quite willing for you to question us as fully as you wish. Question, I said, however," he added with a quick glance at Dorcas. "Not accuse."

There was again a silence as Wait did not immediately reply. Dorcas could not tell whether Jevan's words had im-

pressed Wait as being sincere or the contrary. Probably the
contrary, for finally Wait said: "Thank you very much, Mr
Locke. There will be a number of questions at the inquest.
That is to take place on Monday. You and Mrs Locke will
be expected to attend, naturally, as witnesses."

"*Witnesses!*" cried Dorcas. Jevan flashed her a warning
look and the detective said:

"Yes, certainly. You were one of the last persons to talk
to Drew. Over the telephone, of course. And a sales record
was found at Jacques's dated a year ago and covering the
purchase of a green tweed suit which exactly answers the
doorman's description of the green suit worn by the woman
with Drew that night; this sales record was made out to
you——"

"I——" An almost imperceptible stiffening of Jevan's shoulders warned her again and she checked herself.

"Yes," said Wait. "That will need explanation. Also at the
inquest there will be a taxi driver who picked up a woman
on the Drive at Schumanze Court on the night of the murder and brought her to this address. He can identify the
woman. Wouldn't it be better to tell me the truth?"

Jevan said quickly: "Mrs Locke has told you the truth."

Wait's slender black eyebrows lifted slightly.

"Very well. At the inquest you will be obliged to swear
to your statements. There is something, however, I'd like to
ask you about before the inquest." He walked as gently as a
cat toward Dorcas and stood just above her so his eyes could
plunge straight down into her own. She shrank back a little
in her chair; he must not see the things in her mind. She must
make her eyes blank and uncommunicative. He said unexpectedly: "How much money have you—loaned Ronald
Drew?"

"*Money!*"

"No hysterics, please. Listen. Drew made for years a pre-
carious and somewhat questionable livelihood. But all at once
last fall he began to have money. Sums of cash deposited
to his account at the Stock Bank. Where did he get it?"

Her head was pressing against the back of the chair. She
shot a frantic glance at Jevan, who had not moved, and
cried: "I don't know! I know nothing of his affairs! I gave
him no money. Not a penny."

"When did you first begin to go about with Drew?"

His face now came between her and Jevan; she moistened her lips. "Recently—last November——"

"You began to be seen together," said Wait definitely, "at exactly the time his bank deposits began——"

"Get out!" said Jevan in a voice of seething rage. His face was white and his eyes blazing. "Get out. In thirty seconds I'm going to kick you out."

Wait turned deliberately and looked at Jevan.

"No," he said. "You aren't going to do that. I have a search warrant, and I'm going to be here for some time while I search the house."

Dorcas, her head still pressed rigidly against the back of the chair, watched the two men face each other for a long ten seconds. Then Jevan, white and furious, thrust his hands violently into his pockets. "All right," he said with suppressed savagery. "That's legal and I can't stop you. But I swear, Wait, if one word of what you've just said reaches the newspapers I'll——"

Wait put up one small hand in a deprecating way: "No threats, Locke. No threats."

He turned and went away. Bench anxiously put his head in the door. "He says he has——"

"A search warrant," cut in Jevan shortly. "Let him go through the house."

Feet went through the hall and up the stairs. Dorcas let out a tremulous, half-sobbing breath. Jevan said grimly, his eyes fastened on the door and a tight white line around his mouth: "I'd like to break his neck. The little——"

"Jevan," she cried unsteadily. "The taxi driver will identify me."

He still didn't look at her. "The only thing you can do is stick to denial. Wait still has no proof——"

"He said I gave Ronald——"

"Forget it," said Jevan crisply. And added thoughtfully: "I wonder, though, who was paying Drew for what. Something crooked, you can depend upon that. He never did an honest day's work in his life." He paused again thoughtfully and then added: "But cheer up, Dorcas. Wait's only playing his hunch. I'm sure of that."

Was he? Jevan still looked white and avoided her eyes. And later, when the detective and two plain-clothes men had gone (as they did very soon), went to question Bench as to what rooms they had searched and what they had looked for.

But Bench didn't know.

After that the day went on quietly. The incidents that filled it were important only in retrospect. There were Wait's early morning visit, Marcus' telephone call and the newspapers in which the Drew case was suddenly augmented, gaining, indeed, a sudden weight and momentum which were mysterious and obscurely threatening. Where the day before there had been at the most half a front-page column, there were now two full columns and they were continued onto following pages. Why? said the newspapers.

WHIPPLE HEIRESS OBJECT OF MURDERED MAN'S LAST TELEPHONE CALL, said the *Call*. And went on to demand: "Who Was Mysterious Woman at Drew Apartment?" That night, for the six o'clock edition, were other headlines: WHIPPLE HEIRESS TO TESTIFY—BRIDE TO BE ON STAND.

That day suddenly there were almost no telephone calls from friends. Cary didn't notice it, nor Dorcas, but Sophie did and spoke of it.

"They are beginning to wonder," she said. "And why not?"

It was that day, too, that the woman in the checked coat came to see Dorcas.

Came so mysteriously and as mysteriously disappeared.

That was in the afternoon, sometime after Marcus' telephone call, which came during lunch. It was for Dorcas.

"Dorcas, have you seen the papers?" Marcus began worriedly. "Has Jevan seen them?"

"Yes."

"Yes; well, don't you think—that is, it seems to me—it seems to me something ought to be done about it."

"What?" said Dorcas wearily.

Marcus didn't know.

"But they're going too far," he said helplessly. "However, aside from the papers, is—is everything all right?"

"Y-yes."

"No, no, something's happened. I can tell it by your voice."

"The house was entered last night but again nothing was taken."

"Good God," said Marcus. "Tell me all about it."

When she told him the little she knew, however, he had no

comment to make but instead asked her if she had looked at his reports.

"No. There's not been time."

"Oh. Well—give Cary my regards," he said and hung up.

That afternoon (as much as anything, Dorcas told herself, to escape the haunted anxiety in Cary's lovely troubled eyes) Dorcas went for a solitary, wind-swept walk.

But she could not leave her thoughts behind. The lake when she reached it was as gray as Jevan's eyes and as incalculable.

She was curiously in need of the solitude the wind and stormy lake gave her. Yet the crowding questions that surged so tumultuously and so urgently in her mind were no more capable of analysis and reply than when she was at home, shut inside the four thick walls of the Whipple house. Instead of clarity there was confusion. Had Jevan killed Ronald? She marshaled arguments for and against it—and suddenly in the middle of it was thinking only of a moment in the night. A moment when the man who was her husband had held her in his arms and had gone away.

Spray touched her face and lips and felt cool and lovely upon their sudden warmth.

She turned toward home and did not know she had been followed until she arrived again at her own street and a block away a man, inconspicuous in his slouch hat and raincoat, let his footsteps lag and finally pause altogether on the corner below the house as she turned in again at the gate.

A plain-clothes man, then. Watching them.

Bench opened the door for her.

"A young woman," said Bench, "is waiting. She did not give her name. She's in the small drawing room. She asked to wait."

But there was no one in the small drawing room. No one, either, in the large drawing room.

Bench was incredulous and confused.

"But she *was* here, Miss Dorcas! She insisted on waiting!"

"And she wouldn't give her name?"

"No, Miss Dorcas. But she insisted on seeing you. I know, of course, you are not in to reporters but this young woman," said Bench with simple conviction, "was not a reporter. She——" He lifted a cushion and looked behind a table and said distractedly: "She was small, slender, wore a black-and-white checked coat and a green hat and green scarf. She was a blonde, I believe, Miss Dorcas, very—er—bright hair."

Dorcas shook her head slowly.

When he was out of sight she went back to the small drawing room. No one, of course, was there and there was no clue to her mysterious visitor.

The house was very quiet and shadowy. Outside on a darkening cold corner a man slouched in growing shadows to watch them as a hunter stalks and watches.

Jevan was in the study, Bench said, and she went to find him, overcoming a strange and rather absurd moment of something that was neither embarrassment nor diffidence but was like both.

He was sitting over the long table, with papers all over it. Neatly stacked papers, with typewritten, margined figures and words. He looked up as she entered, squinting as the hard light from above struck full in his face.

"Oh, Dorcas," he said. "Come in. I'm trying to make a start on these things."

These things—oh yes; the brown brief case lay gaping on its side.

She sat down. He leaned back in the chair.

"Bench said someone was waiting to see you."

"Yes. She went away. She wouldn't give her name."

"What's that?" said Jevan sharply and questioned her at length, even going so far as to get up and go prowling through the drawing room and hall as if the woman in the checked coat and green scarf must still be somewhere about. She wasn't of course. Back in the study he laughed a little.

"It was nothing. Somebody wanted a charity subscription —something like that. She got tired of waiting and simply walked out."

He linked his hands together and frowned over them at the reports on the table and told her he had traced the telephone call of the previous night.

"It was Marcus Pett's number," he said.

CHAPTER 14

"Marcus!"

"Yes. He says he didn't telephone. Seemed absolutely astounded. I got him at the club and asked him about it. Says he slept like a top all night and never thought of telephoning here."

"But—are they certain? I mean, the telephone operator. How can they trace a call?"

"I don't know exactly how. I'll find out. But in the meantime I'm pretty well convinced that they were right."

"Marcus—oh, but, Jevan, if he says he didn't telephone, he didn't. He would have no reason——" She broke off abruptly as Jevan's hand made a slight, almost imperceptible little motion toward the laden table. She followed the gesture and looked up directly to seek the answer in his face.

She found it. For he said quietly: "I think you'd better start to work on these reports."

"Marcus is as honest as the day. He's taken care of everything for us for years. He was my father's friend. He——"

"Marcus," said Jevan, "tried to borrow fifty thousand dollars of the Stock Bank two months ago. On his own account. Not yours. Willy's a vice-president there. He found it out today and told me. Marcus was refused."

"That has nothing to do with me or my affairs."

"I hope not," said Jevan heavily. "But there's something else you don't know. And that is . . ." He paused and looked up at the stag and said simply: "The stag, this morning, wasn't quite square and straight with the world."

"What do you mean?"

"Don't be a dunce, Dorcas. I mean the picture had been moved sometime, probably during the night. Probably, too, by our midnight visitor who makes free with the doors and laundry chutes. And who can't come again tonight."

"Jevan, you are implying impossible things. You are saying Marcus——"

"I'm saying nothing except that you ought to examine these reports. And that the picture was moved during the

101

night and these reports had just been placed in the safe."

"But Marcus," Dorcas began and stopped because it simply wasn't possible.

"I know," said Jevan rather grimly. "None of it makes any sense, for it's contradictory. If Marcus—well, call it by its name—if Marcus embezzled he wouldn't insist upon us looking at the reports. He wouldn't bring them to us so promptly and invite us so urgently to examine them and then turn straight around and make a secret entrance into the house at night in order to recover them. Besides, he telephoned from his house—at least someone telephoned from his house—at exactly the time someone was prowling about here last night. Therefore could our visitor have been Marcus? Answer comes there, saying no. But, again contradictorily, the house was entered also the night we were mar—that is, the night before last. Before Marcus had brought his reports. Thus if the reports are the purpose of the nocturnal caller he must have thought the reports were already here at that time. Or——" Jevan stopped, rose, made an impatient turn across the room and said crossly: "Or anything! There's no sense to it. Except I think we ought to look at these reports. And keep them in a better place than the safe. For if Ronald——"

"*Ronald?*"

"Well, suppose Marcus embezzled and Ronald knew of it, threatened Marcus with exposure and Marcus——"

"Marcus murdered him! Oh no!"

Jevan looked at his cigarette.

"No," he said after a moment. "It doesn't seem exactly credible, does it? . . . It may take an accountant to give the reports a thorough check. I've not made a start and it's an accountant's job. It . . ." He paused again, flipped some pages of a sheaf of typewritten papers and said thoughtfully: "Marcus ought to have done that. He ought to have had certified accountants check these figures."

He was right of course. Marcus ought to have done that.

Jevan's hands straightened out upon the papers below them. Good hands, thought Dorcas irrelevantly, well shaped and firm and just now oddly tense looking. He said in a voice that was, however, not at all tense but quite nonchalant and cool: "There's something else I want to say to you, Dorcas. It's about our marriage. I—I can say it all in a moment or two. I realize now that I made a mistake."

"A mistake?"

"Yes. I ought not to have made you marry me as I did. But at the time it seemed the best thing to do—the only thing. In a way it still seems so. But I want you to know that as soon as this thing is over—this trouble about Ronald's murder—I'll go away and we can get an annulment. It can be managed quite simply. . . . That's all, Dorcas."

That's all, Dorcas. A mistake. It can be managed quite simply.

And just then Bench came to the door and said he had reached Mr Devany and he was on the telephone and Jevan murmured an excuse and went to the telephone.

After he had gone she sat for a long time without moving.

The wedding ring on her finger caught a small serene gleam of light. Her throat felt queer and tight. That, then, was the answer. He did not love her. He had married her, yes. He had all but carried her to the altar.

But not for love. Why, then?

She never knew how long it was before the stacks of papers on the table began to thrust themselves upon her attention.

She must return them to the safe. She rose stiffly, as if she'd been sitting there for a long, long time, and went to the table.

Typewritten columns, figures, sheaves of papers clipped together. She made one or two motions to gather the papers together and then sat down and began, abstractedly at first, to look at them. One figure leaped at her out of a maze and had six ciphers and she stared at it, a little frightened and shocked at the weight of social responsibility it implied. As fortunes go her own wasn't staggering; they had always lived quietly, with pleasant, sane simplicity and with the ingrained regard for real values of human conduct of the average American bourgeois household. They used for themselves only what they needed to use of their income; those people who gained livelihood from the wheels that the bulk of that money helped to turn profited as greatly from it as did any member of the family.

It was an interlocking system of mutual dependence and she had been bred to recognize the fact just as she had imbibed, inherent in her upbringing, other ideas of living.

Time passed. Jevan did not come back. Gradually some

of the typed rows began to have meaning for her; now and then she recognized some personal item, an expenditure of her own, Sophie's steady two hundred a month allowance, her mother's larger monthly check; less often a stock transaction looked familiar and she would remember Marcus' mentioning it to her.

It grew dark; the windowpanes at the other end of the room winked and glittered and reflected eerily a long mahogany table and her own cherry-colored sweater and the light shining down on her brown hair, making little gleams of gold in it.

The house grew silent. Once, dimly, through her preoccupation she thought she heard footsteps and a door closing distantly. And later there was a soft shuffle of footsteps again, for she glanced at the door expectantly. The hall beyond was dark and the light from above her head shaded so that it cast a rich pool of light downward but beyond the boundary of that pool it was dusk. She saw no one and the soft shuffle that had attracted her attention did not recur.

It was almost seven o'clock when she looked at her wrist watch. Seven o'clock and dinner at seven-thirty.

Where was everybody? Dressing for dinner, as she must do. But first these reports.

She gathered the papers together and began to stack them quickly, struck with a sudden impatience. It took a moment or two to get the safe open. It opened finally and she thrust the papers inside it, closed the door and twirled the dial. And someone, somewhere, spoke.

It was only a word or two, muffled by the little jar of the door of the safe, and it wasn't very far away.

No one, of course, was in the room.

She went to the door. No one was visible in the hall and a cold current of air struck her face and she saw that the little side door was open; it made a dim grayish rectangle. The passage itself was dark except for the light which streamed into it from the main hall at the other end of it. She went to the side door and closed it.

Someone, carelessly, had left it open. When?

She turned. A path of light from the central hall stretched along ahead of her, outlining blackly the silhouette of a small table against the wall.

She passed the door of the study again and the door of the laundry chute. She passed the telephone room.

Or rather she did not pass it.

For her foot struck something.

It was something soft and yielding—the rug rolled up, a coat dropped, she thought and looked down.

The thing on the floor was dim and white and it was a man's hand.

She must have pulled open the door to the telephone room. For now it was open and, huddled awkwardly, half in and half out the little room, was a black lump that was completely sodden and inert.

It was the man whose hand she had almost trod with her foot and it was Marcus Pett.

She said something and put her hand upon him and jerked it instantly, sharply away.

The fingers were wet and dark and Dorcas screamed.

CHAPTER 15

BENCH, in the dining room, heard that scream and came running with a napkin in his hand.

Dorcas knew that. Then, instantly it seemed, there were lights everywhere. There were people and somebody screamed and began loudly to sob and it was one of the maids. And all at once, too, Sophie was there in the middle of things in a pale green satin negligee with her face, under layers of cold cream, the color of the satin.

Sophie must have taken charge of things, for somebody—Bench—was phoning for the police and Dorcas' voice seemed to be replying to many questions and the replies didn't satisfy Sophie, who pushed her away and cried: "Where's Jevan? Where's Jevan? Bench, where's Mr Locke?"

Nobody knew. And Grayson, the chauffeur, came running heavily through the hall, his coat unbuttoned, his hair awry and wet. "Cook said somebody—oh, my God, it's Mr Pett!"

In an incredibly short time the police got there. Dorcas was huddled on the stairway when they came and hadn't any notion of how she had got there. Probably she had started instinctively to go to her mother and had stopped midway. Mamie was with Cary anyhow; Sophie had ordered her to go to Cary, to tell her anything but the truth. But where was Jevan?

Huge blue figures crowded into the hall; Sophie, holding up her trailing green satin, directed them.

They brushed past her. Sophie and Bench followed them. Cook and the chauffeur and one of the maids, the one who had screamed and burst into tears, stood in a little group, with Cook's face the color of one of her own cream soups. The second girl peered into the little passage and clutched the chauffeur's arm. Her name was Ethel Stone and she was to have that night her one moment of dramatic emergence from obscurity.

Where had Jevan gone? Why was he not there?

Dorcas shut her eyes and leaned her head against the railings and then had to open her eyes again, impelled by a horrible need to watch what was happening below her. No one for a while spoke to her; no one questioned her. The police were busy, here, there, everywhere; men in plain clothes were entering the door, bringing queer paraphernalia, being shown the body, taking pictures of it so flashes of light winked brightly through the hall. Wait was there; a police doctor was there with his bag. Abruptly reporters were at the door and being told to wait. The whole thing to Dorcas was indescribably confusing and she still felt sick and cold with shock.

But in the middle of it Jevan came back. He came hurriedly through the front door and she saw him and cried, "Jevan!" above the pounding of her heart. He didn't hear her. Policemen had fastened upon him and led him instantly into the small drawing room; she had only a glimpse of him. But Willy Devany had followed him into the house and saw her and hurried up the stairs.

He took her hands. "Dorcas, what happened?"

She tried to tell him. Sophie passed below them along the hall, her green satin swishing gently, and disappeared in the little powder room below the stairway. When she came out she had rubbed off the cold cream and her face, up to now grotesque with smears of white cream, looked indecently bare and actually ghastly. She saw them on the stairway and came to join them.

"Jevan was with me," said Willy without being asked. "There was something we wanted to talk about and he phoned me and I met him at the corner drugstore."

"That's neat," said Sophie, looking at her hands, pink and moist as if she had just finished scrubbing them in hot water. "You have an alibi and so has Jevan."

"Yes," said Willy and then caught himself up shortly. "What do you mean, *I* have an alibi? I don't need an alibi."

"Oh, don't you," said Sophie. "Well, that's lucky for you. The rest of us, I think, are in for a bad time." She looked at her hands again and said with curious obliquity: "Dorcas, were you in the little powder room tonight? At any time?"

"No. Why?"

"Nothing," said Sophie and then they saw that Wait was at the bottom of the steps. Willy cleared his throat and got up hesitantly.

"Do you—do you want something?" he said.

"Yes. You."

Willy looked down at Dorcas with troubled, pale blue eyes and then back at Wait. "Oh, all right. But I don't know what you want to question me for. I don't know anything about this."

He leaned over to pat Dorcas' hand and went down to join Wait. They turned into the drawing room and still Jevan did not emerge.

Events telescoped. People came and went and reporters were met at the door and the telephone rang a good deal. Once when the door opened Cary's doctor came into the hall and Sophie looked and exclaimed: "Mamie must have called him. Then Cary knows," and went to meet him. He was curious, darting quick glances everywhere, but was also embarrassed as if he might be somehow and distastefully involved in the thing. He scarcely spoke to Dorcas as he passed her.

At nine o'clock Wait sent for her.

He was by that time in her father's study, sitting on a corner of the long mahogany table. Some policemen were there, one with a notebook. Someone had been smoking—the air was full of smoke; Jevan wasn't there, nor Willy, and over a policeman's broad blue shoulder peered Bench's face, pale and distressed.

A chair was pushed to her.

"Tell me," said Wait, "exactly how and where you found the body."

She did so.

Did so, in fact, not once but many times, all at once conscious of fantastically weak points of her story. A man murdered, his throat not very neatly cut, not more than twenty-five feet from where she sat, and she had known nothing of it.

Not only Wait questioned her; all of them took a hand in it. One of them, a big man in plain clothes, kept asking her about the knife. Where was it? Hadn't she seen it? She must have seen it. Had she moved it? Had she touched it? And, at last, had she hidden it?

"No, no," cried Dorcas. "There was no knife."

The lights were terribly bright. She was terribly tired—so tired that their faces seemed to move, circling around her. She never knew how long it was before the plain-clothes man who kept asking about the knife had his answer.

The answer, however, did not come from her.

There was all at once a commotion in the corridor, a woman's voice, high and thin and excited, heavy footsteps of men. Everyone looked as the core of sounds reached the door and it was the second girl, Ethel Stone, with a policeman at each side. She was excited and there were two bright pink streaks in her cheeks.

"This girl says she knows," began a policeman but the girl broke in.

Ethel Stone: living obscurely an obscure life. Now for one startling, meteorlike moment she emerged into drama. Her very body was shaken and trembling with it and she gave Dorcas a glazed look which did not perceive.

"The knife," she said gaspingly, "wasn't there. And when I went to put out the butter balls there it was again! And there's a wet towel in the powder room."

Bench, in the background, came to life.

"Don't believe her," he cried. "Don't believe a word she says. She doesn't know a thing."

CHAPTER 16

THE GIRL'S EYES, still glazed with excitement, found and fastened upon Wait. She twisted her thin fingers in her apron and cried: "The steak knife. The pantry. I'm telling you the truth." And told her queer little story and played her small but intensely important role.

Unfortunately the grisly little story had the stamp of truth; she couldn't possibly have made it up. Bench, called upon to do so, confirmed it, albeit reluctantly and with a look of cold hatred at the girl.

Bench had got out the silver for dinner as it was his duty to do. They were having steak and among other things he had got out a steak knife and fork; the knife was small and, always, extremely sharp.

"I sharpened it," he said with a smothered gulp. "And put it down on the serving shelf in the butler's pantry."

He had then returned to the kitchen.

"What time was that?" asked Wait.

"I'm not sure. About six, I think."

"Go on."

While he was in the kitchen Ethel had come into the pantry and proceeded on into the dining room to lay the cloth for dinner and to arrange the flowers.

"Roses. Pink ones, they was. And the knife was gone. Everything else was there but the knife was gone."

"Are you sure?"

"Oh yes, Mr Wait. I looked for it. I thought Mr Bench had forgotten it. Everything else we would need was there on the tray but not the steak knife. I looked in the silver drawers for it and didn't find it so I decided that Mr Bench was sharpening it in the kitchen."

"Did you ask Bench about the knife?"

"No sir. I finished the table and went back to the kitchen and started making butter balls. I forgot about the knife. I was busy in the kitchen for—oh, quite a while."

"How long?"

"I don't know exactly. Twenty minutes, I expect. But when

I finished the butter balls and put them in a dish with ice and took them to the pantry serving shelf there—there was the knife again. Beside the fork. Bright and shining with its edge freshly sharpened——"

"Get the knife," said Wait. There was a slight stir as the policeman went away. Wait looked at Ethel again.

"Did you touch the knife?"

"Oh no, sir. I just now remembered it and went to look to be sure the knife was still there and the policeman asked me what I was looking for and I pointed at the knife and told him and he——"

"'Did *you* touch the knife?" Wait asked Bench.

"Not after I got it out and sharpened it, sir. I didn't know it was gone—I don't think it *was* gone. Ethel's trying to make out that somebody took the knife and killed Mr Pett with it and then brought it back again."

Ethel blinked once and said, somehow clinchingly, "And there's a wet towel in the powder room."

It was the second time she had talked of a wet towel. Wait said: "What about it? What do you mean?"

"Well, I mean it's all wet. Soaked in water and wrung out. It's not just damp and spotty and crumpled as if somebody had dried their hands on it. There's several towels in the room; I put out fresh ones in the evening and in the morning. Unless we're having company, when I'm supposed to change them during dinner. Well, I looked in the powder room just now and there's a wet towel there and I think it had blood on it and the blood was washed out. Cold water," said Ethel with those feverish streaks of color burning in her cheeks, "takes out bloodstains."

Someone else that night, thought Dorcas, had talked of the powder room. Someone—Sophie, of course. She had asked her, Dorcas, if she'd been in the powder room that night. Sophie, then, had seen the wet towel, too, had grasped its implications.

A steak knife and a small linen towel. Dorcas knew the steak knife; short, extremely sharp, with a shining, razorlike edge, sturdy and strong as a dagger. A wound such as that one made in Marcus' throat had to be made by something extremely sturdy and strong, something terribly sharp. And even then there would have to be a certain amount of force behind it.

Who would know of the steak knife? The answer, of

course, was: someone in the house. Someone who had seen the knife before. Someone who knew where to find it. Yet —yet couldn't someone who had entered the house—as the murderer of Marcus Pett *must* have done, cried something desperate and frightened in her heart—couldn't some stranger, wanting a knife, have thought of the pantry? Yes, certainly; and he could have watched his chance to enter and there found, obligingly laid out for him by a coincidence that was, really, no coincidence, the very weapon. Short, strong, sharp.

The policeman returned with the knife, holding it gingerly with a scrap of tissue paper. The knife caught a wicked, swift gleam of light.

Wait took it lightly in his fingers and looked at it. Everyone in the room looked, too, as if the thing might speak to them. It was to Dorcas poignantly familiar. How many times had Marcus sat at their table and idly watched the use of that knife! Had he never had a premonition, had he never felt the smallest, faintest chill when that thin blade turned and cut and glittered?

"There's no blood on it," said Wait. "Unless there's some around the handle or in the initial. Might be. Take it to the laboratory, McGill, and get a report as soon as you can."

Everyone watched as the policeman's big hand took the knife. He went out of the room and Wait followed him.

No one knew quite what to do. They waited in unearthly stiffness and stillness until finally Wait returned.

"Bench."

"Yes—yes sir."

Wait looked at Dorcas and said to Bench: "You say that when Pett arrived tonight you opened the door for him?"

"Yes sir."

"What did he say?"

"He came into the house and gave me his hat and coat and stick and——"

"What did he say?"

"Well, he—he said he came to see Madam and I started toward the stairs to announce him when he said not to announce him; that he'd go right up."

"Was this customary?"

"Well, yes and no. Madam often receives her friends in her own drawing room on the second floor——"

"I mean, was it customary not to announce him?"

"No sir. But Mr Pett being almost a member of the family, I thought nothing of it and did as I was told."

"And that was?"

"I put his coat and hat and stick in the closet beside the door and asked if he wished a scotch and soda. He looked very tired and it was his favorite drink. He was in the drawing room at that point, warming his hands over the fire. He said no. Said it sharply and looked annoyed and I went back to the dining room."

"What time was this?"

"I don't know exactly. A little after six, I would say."

"Before or after you had put out the silver for dinner?"

Bench went green around the mouth.

"After."

"What did you do then?"

"I went to the kitchen and went on about my work."

"Was the steak knife on the shelf where you had placed it at the time you went through the butler's pantry?"

"I—I don't know. I don't know, Mr Wait. I didn't notice and that's the truth."

"So the last you saw of Pett, he was standing in the drawing room beside the fire, warming his hands?"

"Yes sir. That's right. Until Miss Dorcas screamed."

"Get Mrs Whipple down here——"

A policeman started toward the door before Wait had finished.

Dorcas cried: "Oh no, please. My mother is ill."

"I'll go up there. I must question her, Mrs Locke. I'll do so in the presence of her doctor, and you, too, if you insist. Look here, Bench; did Mr Pett arrive before or after Mr Locke had gone?"

"After," cried Bench earnestly. "After. I can swear to that. Mr Locke was out of the house and gone fully a quarter of an hour before Mr Pett arrived. And Mr Devany had gone at least two hours——"

"Devany! Was he here this afternoon?"

"Only for a moment, sir. He asked for Miss Whipple—that is, Mrs Locke—and when I told her she was out he said he'd only called to see how she was; that it was nothing important. He went away then."

"Are you sure he went away?"

"Mr Devany?" said Bench in surprise. "Oh yes, sir. His car was waiting and he was driving himself. I saw him get into it and go slowly up the street. It was the woman in the checked coat who didn't——" Light broke in Bench's pale face and he cried eagerly: "*She* didn't leave, sir! At least no one saw her leave! She said she'd wait for Miss Dorcas and then she didn't and——"

"What woman?" snapped Wait and listened to the vague and inconclusive story of the woman in the checked coat. The blond woman in the green hat and scarf who had not waited.

"And you don't know who it was?"

"No."

"And no one saw her leave?"

"She just vanished, sir," said Bench eagerly.

"She's not in the house now, Mr Wait," said the sergeant. "There's nobody at all in the house but the members of the household. We've searched every inch. Shall I put a man on it?"

"Yes, at once. You're got her description. . . . Now then, Mrs Locke, Pett managed your business affairs, didn't he?"

"Yes. Up to now. His trusteeship ended automatically with my marriage."

"Yes, I know. Had he already turned over your property to you?"

"Yes. That is, he had brought all his reports; they are here now. We haven't had time to do anything about his reports yet and we asked him to take care of things until we —until I return from my wedding trip."

"I'd better take those reports. Had you ever had any reason to suppose that Pett was not altogether honest?"

"None. My mother and I would have trusted him with anything we possessed."

"You can't take those reports," said Jevan from the doorway. "You have no right to."

Wait whirled around. "Didn't I tell you to keep him out?"

"I couldn't help it, Mr Wait," said a policeman breathlessly. "He wouldn't stay and short of knocking him out——"

"It wouldn't have hurt him," said Wait morosely. "Look here, Locke, if you and your wife are innocent you can't object to inquiry and you ought to be willing to do everything in your power to help."

"I am," said Jevan unexpectedly. "And I will." He came into the room. He didn't look at Dorcas; she wouldn't have thought that he recognized her presence at all except for the fact that somehow he managed to stand between her and Wait.

"There are one or two things outside your inquiry that might affect it," he said. "I'll tell you what they are. This house has been entered twice, at night. We don't know who entered it or why. Last night somebody telephoned here in the middle of the night; whoever it was telephoned from Marcus Pett's house and Marcus said he didn't. There was what I believe to be an attempt to steal some or all of the reports of Marcus' trusteeship; we are going to have the reports examined by a certified accountant. But we'll do it; not you. You can't object to that. To the best of my knowledge Marcus was absolutely honest but I know he was short of money himself and—why I don't know—tried to borrow some a few months ago. Ask me any questions you want to. But leave my wife out of this."

"I can't leave her out of it," said Jacob Wait after a moment, speaking rather softly. "She's in it and you're in it, Locke. Up to your neck."

There was a stir at the door, interrupting them. Someone said: "Here she is," and Sophie, still in green satin, came slowly into the room, the policeman behind her. She didn't wait for the detective to question her but began to speak immediately.

"Oh, it's you that wants to know about the powder room," she said to Wait. "Yes, I was in the room. And I was in it after the murder while your policemen were all over the house. Why not?"

"Did you wash bloodstains from a towel and hang it over a rod to dry?"

"No," she said instantly. "Certainly not."

Sophie was lying; Dorcas knew it as certainly as she had ever known anything in her life. She remembered Sophie's pink hands, looking as if they had just been scrubbed in soap and water.

Dorcas could not tell whether Wait accepted it or not. He gave Sophie a brief, thoughtful look and went back to Jevan, as if there had been no interruption.

"I'll listen to anything you've got to say. What are your reasons for claiming the house has been entered at night?"

"I'll tell you everything I know," said Jevan and did it fully then and there except that he did not mention Ronald's death or his own and Dorcas' actions on the night of Ronald's murder.

Wait stopped him occasionally to question.

"Pett said he would continue to manage your wife's affairs?"

"For the time being, yes."

"Would you say he leaped at the chance to postpone an inquiry into his reports?"

Jevan hedged. "Not that exactly. He did offer to take the reports away with him."

Once the detective swerved unexpectedly to the woman in the checked coat.

"Do you know who this woman was?"

"I didn't see her."

"Is there anyone connected with either Pett or Drew who would answer the description your man gave us?"

"I couldn't answer that either. Do you mean . . ." Jevan stopped.

Wait said: "If you were going to ask if there's a connection between Drew's murder and Pett's, I would say it is fairly obvious. I don't know yet who killed Drew and I don't know yet who killed Pett. But there is certainly a link." He was looking thoughtfully at Dorcas. He addressed her directly:

"About this business of the telephone call and your experience in the hall that night: did you actually see anyone?"

"No."

"You only heard a sound?"

"Yes. As if the door to the laundry chute had closed."

"I see," said Wait.

It was after that that the detective questioned Cary.

He permitted Dorcas to be present. Dorcas and a man with a notebook who stood in the shadow of the gilded french screen beside the door. Cary lay in the middle of the great bed, with the bedlight shaded from her face, and looked at them.

There were bottles on the bed table and a glass or two and a carafe of water. Cary's little face, surrounded by its soft halo of light hair, was white and still against the smooth pillow. She wore a delicate, lacy bed jacket and her little, slender hands with faint blue veins in them clutched at the edge of the white silk cover which otherwise was without a wrinkle, as if she had not moved since it was adjusted.

She said gently, "Won't you sit down, Mr Wait?"

He did so, in one of Pennyforth Whipple's great, solid arm-chairs. Dorcas hoped he would see at once how small and gentle she was; how fragile and sweet. How utterly impossible it would be for Cary Whipple to hurt anything in the world.

She could discover, however, nothing of this comprehension in Wait's face.

"You knew of the murder then?" he said.

Cary answered instantly. All her replies, indeed, were very prompt, almost taking the words from Wait's mouth.

"Yes. My maid told me. I insisted on knowing what had happened."

"Did you know of the circumstances of the murder?"

"My daughter found him. In the hall leading to the study. A knife . . ." said Cary on a quick breath and stopped.

"When did you first know of the murder?"

"It must have been about seven. A little after seven, for I had just finished dressing and was about to go down when Mamie came. I made her tell me the truth. She sent for my doctor."

"You did not see Pett when he came?"

"Oh no. No. I was here—in my room; I've been here since shortly after five. I—I was resting and then about six I began to dress. I didn't hear anything; I suppose the water was running in my bathroom. Mamie said my daughter screamed——"

"Did you expect Pett to dinner?"

Dorcas tried to take her mother's hand but the little fingers would not relinquish their clutch on the bedcover.

"No, I did not expect him to dinner. I did—expect him, however. He had telephoned to me, you see; I took the call at my telephone here. It was about five o'clock. He—he just said that he was coming. That he wanted to see me."

"Is that all?"

"Yes. Yes, that's all."

"What was it he wanted to talk to you about?"

"But I—I don't know. He didn't say. I have no idea what it was."

"What would you say," said Wait slowly, "if someone suggested that Pett had embezzled money? Your money?"

"You mean Dorcas' money," said Cary. "I would say that he had not. But if he had, he would have told me. He would have known that we would help him to replace it. He would have confessed it to me; I'm sure he would have confessed. Did he"—she turned her little head quickly toward Dorcas —"did he take money, Dorcas? Do they know he did that?"

"We shall know very soon," said Wait at once and Cary's lovely eyes swept back to him. "Mrs Whipple, did you leave the house on any errand at all last Wednesday night?"

"Wednesday night," repeated Cary thoughtfully as if considering it. "*Wednesday night!* But that was the night before Dorcas' wedding!"

"Yes."

"And the night—the night Ronald was—why are you asking me such a question? What has that to do with Marcus?"

"So you did leave the house that night when everyone thought you were in bed?"

"Of course not. Certainly not! Ask anyone. What a question! Do you think *I* shot Ronald?"

The little phrases were as quick and soft as the beat of a bird's wings and had the same tremulous quality. Dorcas could see the feverish beating of a pulse in her mother's soft white throat. She turned rather desperately to the detective.

"Isn't that enough?" she cried.

He did not even look at her. He did, however, rise and stand looking at Cary for a moment before he said quietly: "I wish I could persuade you to tell me whatever it is that you—don't want to tell. Don't make the mistake of trying to shield someone."

For a moment Cary did not reply. Instead she shrank into her soft pillows, shrank into her lacy bed jacket, shrank into the heretofore protected haven of the great bed. Shrank like a terrified child with her great blue eyes fastened on Wait and unexpectedly, with her eyes wide-open, began to cry.

"I've done nothing," she sobbed in tremulous little gusts. "Dorcas has done nothing——"

"You've made her ill," said Dorcas furiously, finding a lacy handkerchief on the table and thrusting it into Cary's little fingers, unloosed at last.

"I've done nothing of the kind," said Wait. "Will you come with me now, Mrs Locke? Ring for her maid if you don't wish to leave her alone."

"Go, Dorcas," said Cary, crying. "Go, dear."

At the door Wait looked at the uniformed policeman who

stood, tablet in hand, in the shadow of the french screen.

"Did you get all that?"

"Oh yes, Mr Wait. Every word."

At the stairway Wait stood aside politely, allowing Dorcas to precede him.

CHAPTER 17

IT WAS THEN nearly midnight.

It was after two o'clock when he left the house.

Almost immediately the next morning it became apparent that with the murder of Marcus Pett the Drew-Pett murder case leaped to the status of a cause célèbre. It was a natural, indeed an inevitable, development. For three days now the Drew murder had been simmering with constantly increasing ebullience and the murder of Marcus Pett had the effect of removing an already trembling lid.

There was an all too obvious connection between the two murders. Marcus Pett's only orbit and one of Ronald Drew's several orbits touched at one tangential point and that tangential point was Dorcas. Mrs Jevan Locke. The former Dorcas Whipple. Or, more frequently, the "Whipple Heiress."

That was the view of the newspapers. The view, reluctant, stunned but inevitable, of the people she knew; the view, apparently, of thousands of people she would never know, who clamored for news and more news, who snatched extras as soon as they came on the street, who planned to attend the trial and made bets as to the outcome.

That night a siege of reporters began which did not for an instant relax. It was like a barrage around the house and grounds. If anyone came, if anyone went, if anyone so much as approached a window to raise or lower a shade there were reporters to see it; reporters to take pictures, reporters to pounce upon and make a news story of whatever material they could ferret out and to fill columns and columns of fine black print with it. It was their duty and they were acting under orders; they were never malicious and there was a detached, impersonal technique of strategy.

Yet the very next morning, Sunday morning, the *Call* said:
WHIPPLE HEIRESS CHARGED WITH MURDER.

"There'll be grounds for enough libel suits to last the rest
of your life," said Jevan grimly. "Don't read them, Dorcas.
Here, Bench, take these papers and burn them."

He took the paper out of her hand but not before she had
seen the headline. And a picture of herself, an old picture in
her debut gown of white silk. She'd carried scarlet camellias, she remembered, and her mother had been lovely and
gracious in soft green lace and Marcus, beaming, had supplied
the camellias.

That was the next morning, late, over breakfast in her own
room, with Jevan striding up and down, smoking and saying
very little. And church bells from the Midway, the carillon,
tolling distantly.

They had said what there was to say the night before.
Wait and his immediate cohorts had left about two. They
had, in the end, made no arrest. There remained, however—
exactly why Dorcas didn't know, except that it seemed to be
customary—a police guard in and around the house. It ought
to have given them a feeling of security. Yet long after Dorcas had finally gone to sleep she roused again; dawn must
have been at hand, for there was a grayish tinge at the windows and in the cold dawn Jevan was sleeping, stretched out
in a bathrobe and an eiderdown on a chair near her with his
long legs on another chair. He was sound asleep; she could
tell it by his regular breathing. Yet he was solidly and firmly
placed between her and the door. It gave her, in the stillness
of that chill and desolate hour, the most extraordinary sense
of comfort and she went straight back to sleep again. But
later in the morning, much later, when she waked to find
Mamie at her bedside with hot coffee, there were no signs of
Jevan's presence. The chairs had resumed their customary
places, and the eiderdown and Jevan were gone. And when
he came into the room, freshly shaven and dressed, he did
not mention it. And she could not. As she could not say:
"Jevan, did you kill Ronald? Jevan, did you—*could* you
have killed Marcus?" But he couldn't have done it; no matter
what reasons he might have had, *he couldn't have done it*.
Not Jevan. She clung to that.

And she couldn't say either: "Jevan, why did you marry
me?"

He had already, early that morning, talked over the tele-

phone to a friend who was a member of a firm of certified
accountants and had given, sealed, into the hands of a West-
ern Union messenger the whole bulk of Marcus' reports.
It would be, he supposed, another day before they could expect definite news of that.

Mamie knocked and came in. Mr Devany was downstairs,
wanting to see Mr Locke.

Jevan went away. And Dorcas, her very muscles aching
with fatigue, dragged herself through the motions of dressing and went to see her mother. Mamie was darning stockings in a chair just outside her mother's door.

"I wouldn't go in if I was you, Miss Dorcas. Your mother
is asleep." She stabbed a stocking heel viciously with her
needle. Mamie looked old that morning. Her usually neat,
grayish hair had wisps down the back of her neck and her
round, Irish face seemed to have sagged. She sat with her
chair against the wall and commanded a long view of the corridor.

"All right, Mamie," said Dorcas and wandered back to her
own room.

It was then late in the morning, nearly noon. A dark morning again and very cold, as if there were no such thing as
spring and never would be.

Her face in the heavy mirror over the dressing table was
pale as a ghost. Absently, automatically she reached for lipstick, selecting a shade at random. The stick of paste felt
strange to her lips and she looked at it abruptly. It—and
every other lipstick in the tray—had been neatly cut off.
The used ends, instead of being smooth and tapering, were
straight and blunt with fine edges, as if the cutting instrument, whatever it was, had been extremely thin and sharp.

Mamie hadn't done it. Who then? Why?

After a moment she thrust the small tubes of varied colors
and shapes back into the drawer and closed it hurriedly and
left the room. She would find Jevan, Sophie, anyone. It
wasn't good, that day, to be alone. Sophie was in the lower
hall, speaking to Bench.

"I don't care if she has given notice, she can't go." They
were talking of Ethel, it seemed, who had decided to leave.
Sophie, seeing her, dismissed Bench.

"Have you seen your mother?"

"She is asleep."

Sophie nodded with satisfaction. "Your mother is showing

unexpected reserves of strength. The doctor was quite satisfied; said he would drop in today if we called him but not otherwise. Your mother is stronger than you realize."

The hall was quite empty. Dorcas leaned forward. "Sophie, what about that towel? You know. Last night. You knew something about it, didn't you?"

"Certainly. I washed it out."

"But why?"

"Sh-h-h. Because there were bloodstains on it, of course. I suppose that damned knife was wiped off on the towel."

"Why, then——"

"Do you think I wanted Wait to have another link between the murder and us? You. Me. Your mother. Jevan."

Bench came through the dining room and into the hall. Dorcas started back at sight of him, as if she and Sophie had been conspiring. He went on to the front door; the bell had evidently been rung. Sophie said: "Jevan's in the conservatory," and went toward the kitchen. Funny, thought Dorcas; meals went on, and a semblance of a domestic routine. Thanks to Sophie, however, who never quite lost her head.

Bench, at the door, was saying no one was at home. Probably a reporter.

She went to the conservatory. Still called the conservatory, though the plants in which Pennyforth Whipple had taken great pride (or had pretended to take pride, according to the fashion at that time) had dwindled to some scraggly-looking banana trees and sparse foliage plants much veined in red. There lingered, however, about the little room with its glassed roof and concrete floor covered with matting the dampish, earthy smell of all greenhouses. Jevan was there, sitting in a wicker chair, and Willy Devany was pacing around and around the small green bronze fountain in which water hadn't run for years. As she opened the french door from the library Willy said cheerlessly:

"Hello, Dorcas," and Jevan said: "You're in good time; I want you to tell me—and Willy, too, of course—everything you remember about that night Ronald was killed. Tell it carefully and put in everything. Willy is all right; don't mind him. It seems to me that there was something in what you told me that made a sort of discrepancy with what I knew. I can't remember exactly what but—well, go ahead, Dorcas. If you don't mind."

She did mind. Telling Willy wasn't, queerly, the same as

telling Jevan. She hated it but she told it. Willy kept on pacing and managing to look disheveled in spite of his always perfect grooming. "She oughtn't to have gone," he kept saying in worried, blue-eyed asides to Jevan. "She oughtn't to have gone."

"Well, she did go," said Jevan finally in an annoyed way. "Do shut up, Willy, and listen. Stop pacing."

"I can't," said Willy distractedly. "Go on, Dorcas. So you put down your cigarette——"

"I can't remember what I did with my cigarette. I can't remember anything about it. I just remember Ronald answering the telephone"—Jevan looked at Willy just then and Willy looked back at Jevan—"and I went away. I hurried. I don't think anyone saw me leave and I hailed a taxi over on Lake Shore Drive and came home. It's that taxi driver that Wait says he's found and will identify me——"

"The whispering in the kitchen and the door opening must have been——" began Willy and Jevan cut him short.

"She doesn't know any more about it than that. She decided the whispering must have been just ice being crushed, although I must say, Dorcas, I can't see much similarity——"

"You would if you had been there. The kitchen is some distance from the living room, along a little hall. And the door that closed—I mean that I thought I heard close—must have been just the—the refrigerator door. And the white door that Ronald closed between the hall and the living room —well, I'm not certain about its moving either. Perhaps I only imagined it; all those mirrors give a queer feeling of motion about you."

"Yes," agreed Willy, adding quickly, "Mirrors have that trick. Didn't you see anyone? Wasn't there anything more— more definite?"

"Nothing. Except there was a car that drew up just behind us as we arrived and it—well, a car had passed slowly as Ronald and I left this house. And then again, later, when I got home and got out of the taxi a car was just leaving—or at any rate it looked like it, although so far as I know no one had called." She looked at Willy, whose face was a blank.

Jevan snapped his fingers impatiently. "I can't find it. There was something and I didn't see it at the time and now I can't —can't get it. What time was it when you reached home, Dorcas?"

"I don't know exactly. I met Ronald at eight. It couldn't have been more than nine-thirty when I got home again."

"I was at the club about that time. I reached Ronald's flat about fifteen minutes later."

Willy made another turn and said to Jevan: "What exactly did you do in Ronald's place? You wiped off the revolver and put it by his hand. You told me that."

"Yes. And I put his fingerprints on it," said Jevan. "It wasn't as easy as it sounds and I expect I smudged them or got the—the fingers in the wrong position somehow and Wait, curse him, spotted it. Then I looked around and wiped off the doorknobs and the telephone and the glass with the lipstick on it and took the three cigarettes that had lipstick on them and——"

"My lipstick!" cried Dorcas. "Every lipstick I have is cut sharply off and the ends are gone."

They received it in a kind of deep silence and she became a little frightened, perceiving that silence.

Then Jevan said sharply: "It means that I overlooked a cigarette somewhere and they found it and are trying to match lipstick on it with one of your lipsticks. But there were only three in the room. Think, Dorcas; are you sure you weren't in any other room? You didn't go to the kitchen and drop the cigarette you were smoking?"

"No. I'm sure of that."

Willy said quickly: "Jevan, isn't it possible that Wait found somewhere else in the apartment a cigarette that somebody else had smoked and left with—with lipstick on it?"

"Somebody," said Jevan and looked at Willy and instantly agreed: "That's it of course. The—whoever it was in the kitchen. If anybody—a woman . . ." Jevan paused thoughtfully.

"A woman," said Willy significantly and Jevan said:

"Heaven send it's not the same lipstick Dorcas uses."

"It couldn't be," observed Willy cheerfully. "There must be hundreds of lipsticks."

"Here's Bench," said Jevan shortly, and Bench rattled the french doors and opened them.

"Mr Wait is here," he said, unpleasantly apropos. "He wants to see——"

"I'll come out there," said Wait behind him and did so. Jevan said quickly: "You'd better go, Dorcas."

"No, Mrs Locke, stay right here. You, too, Devany. I

think you ought to know that Marcus Pett's accounts are nearly a hundred thousand dollars short."

"Short!" cried Jevan incredulously. "You can't know! I only sent off the reports this morning."

"Telephone your friend if you don't believe it. I've just left him. You chose a very good man, Locke, one who knew how to spot a shortage. He said it was as plain as the nose on my face," observed Wait a trifle grimly.

"But there hasn't been time for him to check those reports!"

"Pett had made no attempt to falsify. He had, in fact, almost pointed it out to you if you had looked in the right place."

"A hundred thousand!" repeated Jevan in a stunned way. "That's an awful lot of money. What on earth did Marcus do with it?"

Wait knew. "Stock market," he said succinctly. "He seems to have tried—by the use of your money, Mrs Locke—to build up a fortune for himself. It's been going on for some time and instead of retrieving losses he got in deeper and deeper. You must have guessed."

He paused but only for an instant, as if to arrange the things he intended to tell them; it gave them no time for exclamations or denials or inquiry but only for acceptance. He went on, making of each sentence a neat, detached fact like links in a chain.

"Two days before Drew was shot he wrote a note to Pett saying he was afraid of someone; the note was found among Pett's papers this morning."

"Who——" began Jevan but Wait went on as if he had not heard it.

"The inquest which was to have taken place tomorrow has been postponed; consequently I have asked the taxi driver who took a woman to this address the night of Drew's murder to come here and identify"—he paused there and looked at Dorcas and said simply—"her. He will be here shortly."

Again Jevan tried to interrupt and Willy, who had disappeared behind a banana plant, uttered a protesting, small sound. Wait went on.

"You, Locke, and you, Devany, have not the alibi for the time last night when Pett was murdered that you claimed to have. You were observed by the clerk in the drugstore, who says you arrived at the store separately, Locke first,

Devany a little later. That was a little before seven o'clock.
You had Coca-Colas, talked for about ten minutes and left
the store together. Locke, you said you left the house (and
Bench corroborates it) a little before six o'clock. That's an
hour, during which you have no alibi."

"I was walking," began Jevan. "Believe it or not——"

"You had plenty of time, then, to return to the house un-
observed by way of the side door, murder Pett, escape again
by the side door and reach the drugstore in time to meet
Devany; the store is not more than five minutes walk from
here."

"You would have to prove——"

"The drugstore clerk also heard part of your conversation.
Who is the woman in the checked coat and where is she?"

CHAPTER 18

"I," SAID JEVAN, "I don't know."

"You talked of her; you said she had been here at the
house; you and Devany agreed she must be found. Now then,
who——"

Jevan's jaw and eyes looked savagely stubborn. "I don't
know, I tell you."

Wait whirled to the banana plant and Willy's anxious blue
eyes blinked frantically. "I don't know her," he cried. "She's
nothing to me. It was only because we thought it was queer
—her coming like that and then disappearing. We thought we
ought to investigate it."

"What did you do after you left the drugstore? It was at
least eight-thirty when you turned up here."

Willy shot a worried look at Jevan, bit his lips and said
jerkily that they had sat in his car and talked.

"For an hour and a half?"

"Yes," said Willy. "And I can swear to it and so can Jevan.
Then we came back to the house and saw lights everywhere
and police and naturally said we'd been together. Self-preservation," said Willy breathlessly. "That's all. I don't know
who in hell that woman is——"

The detective turned back to Jevan.

"I wonder," he said simply and directly, "if you quite real-ize the motives which we feel might have led to the mur-der of Ronald Drew and subsequently to Pett's death. Lis-ten to me. Suppose your wife (who was not then your wife) was threatened by Drew. Wait, let me finish! Suppose he in-tended to throw a monkey wrench into the wedding plans and told her so; suppose she went to his apartment in the hope of inducing him to give up his plan—perhaps she meant to pay him off. Suppose you learned of it and followed her. Suppose you realized that he would go on demanding money and there was only one way to stop it. Certainly someone had already been paying him regularly for no apparent value received and there is only one person close to Drew who had the money to make such payments and conceivably the motive——"

Dorcas' heart was throbbing painfully in her throat. Jevan shot her a lightning look and said, evenly enough except for a deep undertone of fury: "It doesn't happen to be true, Wait. It's only a theory."

"But it does fit," said Wait. "Especially if we suppose that Marcus Pett, in charge of your wife's money, knew of these payments, knew of a motive for Drew's murder and in fact knew so much that he, too, had to be murdered."

Jevan was white to the lips; he said, however, still evenly: "It's still theory only."

"Theory? More than that, Locke." He looked at his watch. "More than theory. The taxi driver ought to be here any moment now."

Dorcas felt queerly cold. How could she have gone so blindly with Ronald; how could she have done the thing that, now, was to tell so fatally against Jevan and against her-self! She wished with the cruel futility with which people have so wished since time began that she could undo the thing she had done. That she could have that last instant of decision over again. But how could she have known how important that short ride with Ronald was to be!

Jevan's face was like a mask except for its tenseness; be-hind it, she knew, he was seeking desperately for a way out, conscious as she was of the danger of the taxi driver's identi-fication. Willy, still shrinking behind the banana plant, stared blankly at the detective. And Bench just then appeared in the doorway, and with him a man in uniform who could be no other than the taxi driver.

He held his cap in his hand; that night she hadn't seen his face; it had been shaded by his cap. She sought for and could find no familiar line. But he had seen her fully; there had been a light on her face from the street lights, and he had leaned toward her and stared a little, noting, she had been sure, her breathlessness and agitation.

She realized that her fingers were digging into the wicker arms of the chair she sat in and that Wait saw it; she tried to look unconcerned, certain of herself, but her face felt stiff and marked with guilt. Jevan had not moved, nor Willy.

Wait looked at the taxi driver and said: "Well?"

He saluted Wait cheerfully: "Here I am, Mr Wait. On the dot. And this is the address all right." He looked at Dorcas. Jevan started and stopped. Dorcas forced herself to meet the taxi driver's eyes. He stared, tipped his head first on one side and then the other, gave Wait, Jevan and Willy a sweeping look, stared again at Dorcas and said cheerfully: "But that's not the girl."

As if released, Dorcas' heart began to thud furiously. She was only dimly aware that Wait, Jevan, the taxi driver and, incredibly, Willy were all talking at once. Out of the melee of voices suddenly one voice, rich and passionate, began to swear. It was Wait's voice and it emerged from and drowned out other voices and grew, gathering strength as it waxed into a stream of Old Testament cursing that blasted them all root and branch.

Willy shrank back behind the banana leaves and looked as if he expected them to begin to shrivel, and Jevan's hand was on Dorcas' arm and she realized he was telling her to go. But she couldn't have moved if her life had depended upon it. She listened; they all listened as if fascinated until suddenly the taxi driver swallowed hard a few times and broke into that rich stream with the hardihood of his profession.

"You ain't got no call to do that," he shouted. "I'd be ashamed if I was you. And on Sunday too."

Wait abruptly stopped. He looked at the taxi driver, looked at Dorcas, looked at Jevan. All at once he smiled; it was a remarkable smile which would have passed for a snarl anywhere.

"You murdered Drew, Locke," he said. "You're guilty as hell."

And turned around and walked out. He passed within an inch of the taxi driver's nose and vanished. The taxi driver said coolly: "And what a nice guy he is," looked at Dorcas and winked deliberately and in the friendliest way. "I guess I'll be going now," he said.

They didn't have the forethought to question him. He disappeared, too, and Jevan belatedly caught the implication of the wink and cried: "Hey, there, wait a minute."

"No, don't stop him," said Dorcas. "I know it's the man. He had a cap on but——"

Willy came out from the banana plant.

"He winked," he said. "Well I'm damned. Chivalry."

"Jevan, Wait didn't mean what he said," began Dorcas. "He couldn't have meant it. You didn't kill Ronald. He can't prove it. He——"

Jevan said coolly, as if there had been no anguish and fear in her voice: "Of course not. Forget it. Willy, what did we say in the drugstore yesterday? What did that soda jerker hear?"

"Just what Wait asked us about, I imagine," said Willy worriedly. He wiped his pale forehead with a very handsome handkerchief and said: "We said we must find the—the woman. And if you'll take my advice, Jevan, you'll get yourself a lawyer. You know I won't—tell—won't tell anything," said Willy. "But they keep questioning me. I might break down."

"You were there too," said Dorcas, suddenly believing it. "You were at Ronald's apartment——"

Jevan interrupted brusquely.

"Willy was not in Ronald's apartment. But for heaven's sake, Willy, can't you—can't you resist Wait? Don't let him bluff you."

"Bluff? Oh, my God, Jevan," cried Willy with the candor of an old friend. "Don't be a plain damn fool. The man's got something on you. You—you didn't kill Ronald, did you? I mean—I mean it's all right if you did. I don't care. He needed killing and you were the man to do it but—you'd better tell me."

"Tell you," began Jevan and stopped short and said: "Just what would you do?"

Willy's answer was simple. "Get a good defense lawyer of course. Herbert is the best criminal lawyer in the country. Shall I wire for him now?"

"No," said Jevan tersely. "And get this into your head. I——" He stopped again, looked at Willy with a kind of helplessness and said: "Oh, never mind. We've got to find that woman."

Willy blinked and said: "Oh yes, certainly but——"

Dorcas thought, What woman? The one in the checked coat of course; yet her brief, almost chimerical appearance did not, surely, justify so deep an interest.

"You see," said Jevan, "it's the cigarette. The cigarette that was smoking when I reached Ronald's apartment. I just now, while Wait was talking, saw what I didn't see before, and that is that it wasn't your cigarette, Dorcas; it couldn't have been, for you had been gone from the apartment for at least half an hour. And that cigarette, as well as two other ends I destroyed, had——"

"Had lipstick on it," cried Willy excitedly. "I'll go! I'll go at once, Jevan! Immediately!" He took a leaf from Wait's book and was about to disappear promptly if abruptly through the door when he stopped, looked back at them, said mysteriously and still excitedly: "The end justifies the means," and was gone.

Dorcas tried to assort it intelligently: "You mean that another woman was in Ronald's apartment after I had gone? And that the woman was the girl who came here yesterday. . . ."

"Perhaps. But I don't know who she is," said Jevan definitely. Too definitely. What was it that Willy and Jevan knew of this woman that they refused to tell her?

Jevan gave her no chance to ask; he said without warning:

"You have never asked me exactly why I came to Ronald's apartment. After, that is, our first . . ." He hesitated and said: ". . . talk. I had as good a chance to murder Ronald as anyone had. For all you know I had as strong a motive. Have you considered whether or not I might have killed him? Tell me the truth, Dorcas."

There was a small deep silence in the little controversy.

Dorcas said slowly, not knowing what her words were to be until she heard them: "Do you believe that I killed him?"

His eyes narrowed a little but continued to look deeply into her own. "You know I thought so at first; what else could I think?"

"And—now?"

"Well, now I don't think so."

"But, believing I had shot Ronald, you still were willing to marry——"

"Marry you! I think willing is the wrong word. As I remember, I rather insisted upon it." He had caught the words from her lips. Now he paused for an instant and replied, indirectly and brusquely: "Whatever else there is—or there is not—between us, you are my wife. And before the world I—well, I hold you as such."

She could not read his eyes. All at once the moment was tinged with portent and its meaning concerned only the two of them. The house and all its concerns were remote and inconceivably distant from them.

Around her was the smell of the warm, earthy little conservatory. In the distance, blurred, was the mellow sound of an automobile horn; the light failing through wavy old glasses was faintly green and very clear upon Jevan's face. It was as if the moment's passage of time lifted itself out of that very passage and became transfixed and would remain so, clear and inviolate forever.

"You haven't answered my question. You haven't told me why you've been loyal to me; why you've told no one that I was in the apartment and found him there? Why you've obeyed me when I've told you what to say and do? And you've——" Jevan broke off and his eyes searched her own and he said, half whispering: "Dorcas, if I killed Ronald—if I was driven then to kill Marcus—would you still trust me?"

Queer how extraordinarily difficult it was to speak; it was as if she had to guard her tongue against saying too much and yet she had no words. And she must reply; he took her hands and compelled her to speak.

"I—I have felt that we stood—together," she said fumblingly, falteringly—stupidly, she thought, and ineptly.

He held her hands for an instant longer and then dropped them.

"Partners in crime?"

"No. I am your wife." She hadn't intended to say that. She caught herself quickly but could not catch back the thing she'd said. He looked at her queerly and smiled.

"My wife. And you want our marriage to be annulled at the first possible moment. . . . Very well." He turned toward the door. "It's lunchtime, I suppose," he said in a different voice, quite cool and detached. "We'd better go in."

He went to the french door and Dorcas followed. There was a shallow step leading upward into the library and as Jevan stepped upon it and put his hand on the latch of the door Dorcas said: "But I do trust you. It's you that said our marriage must be annulled." He whirled instantly toward her, eyes so bright that she faltered and added unsteadily: "If you killed Ronald——"

He thrust the door shut and took a quick step toward her. "Well? If I killed Ronald . . . ?"

It was terribly important. She looked up at Jevan and tried to speak, though she did not know what she was about to say. And she did not ever say it, for without any warning at all he took her fiercely in his arms and her faltering words were muffled as he kissed her. Kissed her and held her so tight that her very body merged into his own strength and warmth; and kissed her again; and everything else in the world became nonexistent and immensely unimportant.

Until all at once he was standing away from her, looking down at her. She was trembling and tried not to. But he knew it and was going to take her into his arms again and she swayed a little toward him in a faint, lovely gesture she learned at that very instant and did not know she learned.

Yet he did not. Instead he said in an odd, rather harsh voice: "You are my wife, you know," and walked again to the door. "Better come to lunch," he said over his shoulder.

The casualness of it was like cold water in her face. And at the same time she thought: When Ronald held me in his arms it was not like this. I hated that. I feared it. I wanted only to escape.

He waited a moment at the door, without looking back toward her. And Dorcas, still shaken and confused, thought, But Ronald loved me. (Or did he?) And Jevan doesn't. He wants our marriage to end. So then it's—it's only chemistry.

"What's that?" said Jevan abruptly as if she'd spoken and Dorcas, absently, still confused, said, "Chemistry," and instantly could have bitten her tongue.

For Jevan looked at her then, quickly, exclaimed, "Chemistry!" and she saw understanding come into his eyes and felt a hot wave start at her throat and surge upward.

"Chemistry," he said again and laughed shortly. "Call it that if you like but come on."

She went and he said no more. Did not, during lunch, so much as look at her. Yet she was absurdly aware of every word he spoke and every motion he made, as if there were fine strong wires between them.

After lunch Jevan disappeared. She saw him in the hall with his coat on and Bench handing him a hat. He went out without seeing her on the stairway or at least without coming to speak to her, and she went on upstairs to her room—rather to the room she had come to after her marriage. With Jevan in the adjoining room.

She closed the door. There were things she must think of; yet when she tried she could not, for those very things kept repeating themselves as experiences. Jevan's mouth, hard and warm upon her own. His arms. "You are my wife," he had said.

Sunday. A quiet, dark afternoon with Cary silent in her room and Mamie sitting outside the door with the Sunday papers and a deep, growing perplexity in her Irish face. With the servants in the kitchen reading avidly all the papers they could get hold of and Ethel getting feverish little red streaks in her thin cheeks again as she saw her own name, Ethel Stone, actually in print.

With Dorcas shutting herself in with thoughts that refused to be thought. Wandering restlessly about the room she had entered as Dorcas Locke. Going once into Jevan's room, a little timidly picking up the brushes on the dressing table, marked J. L. in solid block initials, and putting them down again.

But it was then that she found the green scarf. An edge of it, a bright green line, was showing in a book on the bed table and without at all meaning to she opened the book and pulled out the small scarf.

Bright green, thin silk, exuding perfume. A heavy perfume, musky. It was a little wrinkled and untidy and there was the smudged mark of lipstick on it.

A woman in a checked coat, Bench had said, with a green hat and scarf. And Jevan had said he didn't know her. And Willy had gone to find her.

She still had the scarf in her hand when Bench came to call her to the telephone. He saw the scarf as she thrust it back into the book and his eyes leaped but he said nothing and she followed him to the telephone.

It was dusk by that time and Bench had turned on all available lights but the little passage outside the telephone room was yet too dimly lighted. She wondered suddenly if Marcus could have been trying to reach the telephone when he was murdered. Or had there been, as was more likely, a ruse on the part of the murderer which led him into the little room so that, sitting, his hands at the telephone, he had been taken by surprise?

She took up the waiting instrument. Her first thought had been that it was Jevan. But it was Wait.

"Mrs Locke, ask your mother why Ronald Drew was afraid of her."

"My mother!"

"Yes, of course. He said so, as I told you this morning, in a letter to Marcus Pett. I have the letter if you want to see it. I'll be along in the morning to hear what your mother says."

"No. You are mistaken. This is preposterous——"

He had hung up before she began. She put the telephone down and with grisly immediacy it rang again. This time she answered it herself and it was, to her great relief, Willy. He recognized her voice.

"Oh, Dorcas—is Jevan back yet?"

"No."

"Well, when he comes tell him Elise is gone. Vamoosed. Nobody knows what happened to her."

"Elise!"

"Completely gone," said Willy's voice thinly and at a great distance. "Checked coat, green scarf and all. Tell him, Dorcas."

He hung up too, quickly, as if he were in a great hurry.

She stood at the telephone. And in the soft, deep dusk she heard from the corridor beyond the swish of a garment and the little stir of someone moving.

CHAPTER 19

SHE WAS a little frightened; and it was ridiculous because it was only Cary.

A Cary who, with equal absurdity, seemed almost as frightened as Dorcas. For she cried nervously: "Dorcas, where are you? Who was it on the telephone?"

"Nobody," cried Dorcas in a gust of relief. "Nobody. That is, it was Willy. Mother, I thought you were upstairs resting."

"I—I came down," she said. "Where was his body? Here?"

Her small feet were almost on the spot. Dorcas put her arm around her mother and turned her toward the wall.

"Come, dear. There's a fire in the library."

Cary permitted herself to be led, but questioned with gentle, stubborn insistence.

"But who was on the telephone? Before Willy, I mean. I—I couldn't help hearing. You said something about me, Dorcas. What was it?"

"Nothing. It—it was only a silly question of the detective——"

She could feel her mother's slender body stiffen.

"The detective! About me? What, Dorcas? You must tell me what——"

"I will. It was nothing, really, dear." (What had she said? What had her mother heard?) "It's only that Wait says he found a note that Ronald had written to—to Marcus, saying he was afraid of you. That's how silly it was. As if anyone could be afraid of you."

Cary did not smile. She put one lovely, fragile hand over her eyes and said after a moment: "Poor Ronald. Dorcas, there's something I want you to promise me."

"Of course, dear. Anything."

Cary hesitated. "Wait until you hear." Her lovely blue eyes had suddenly a kind of feverish light that reminded Dorcas fleetingly of Willy's eyes when he had told her he loved her.

"If they—the police, I mean," said Cary, "accuse you of the murder of Ronald——"

"But, Mother——"

"You are to tell me. At once. Before they make an arrest. Promise." Gentle, stubborn. Helplessly Dorcas agreed and thought that the childish futility of it was like Cary.

"Thank you, dear," said Cary.

That was all. Sophie came down presently with a cigarette in one hand and Sunday newspapers in the other. She put the papers down.

"When this thing is over," she said, "we'll have to start getting an entirely new set of servants. Cook gave notice too. I've been looking at the want ads. Wages are going up."

Cary sighed. And it was only a few moments after that Jacob Wait came in. He asked for Dorcas and waited for her

in the little front dining room and there was a man with him.
A second taxi driver.

Who promptly, in a rather bored but positive enough way,
told Wait that at a little after nine o'clock on the night of
March eleventh he had taken her as a fare from the corner
of Lake Shore Drive and Schumanze Court to the Whipple
house.

"You are certain it's the same woman?"

"Sure it's the same woman. She was upset, looked as if she'd
been running. All excited and flustered. Could hardly tell
me the number of the house. Sure I remember."

"Thank you," said Wait. "That's all." The taxi driver was
looking at the marble head and Wait said more sharply:
"You can go now."

Bench quickly opened the door and the taxi driver was
gone. Wait said, his eyes looking very lustrous: "You see,
Mrs Locke? They found him late this afternoon and had
him waiting for me when I reached headquarters just after I
telephoned you. It changes things. For now you are going to
tell me the whole truth. You were the woman with Drew in
his apartment."

She was beaten and he knew it. She took a long breath and
said yes.

Wait was brisk, businesslike and not unkind. But when she
had finished that story there was nothing he did not know.
Nothing, that is, of her own actions on the night of Ronald's death. She did not mention Jevan.

It was difficult when he questioned her minutely about
the glass she had taken in her hand.

"You say you drank from the glass?"

"Yes."

"That was in the living room of the apartment?"

"Yes. I was in no other room."

"Were you wearing gloves?"

"No."

"There were no fingerprints. Did you wipe your fingerprints off the glass?"

"No. Ronald was alive when I went away, just as I've told
you. There was no need for me to think of removing fingerprints."

"Why did you go to the kitchen? You haven't told me that.
A cigarette end was in the kitchen and it was stained with lip-

stick. There was a glass there, too, with a little whisky remaining in it. And again no fingerprints."

"But I wasn't in the kitchen. And I've told you that I thought—thought someone else was there."

"I'm going to put my cards on the table," he said then. "I told you I had a note which Ronald had written to Marcus. I have and here it is."

He took the note from a pocket and gave it to her to read. It was in Ronald's ornate handwriting and on Ronald's paper and read simply: "Dear Marcus: Things are okay except for the money. I must have more but I promise results." It was signed "R" and below the signature was a scrawled postscript: "Am beginning to be afraid of Cary."

"'Am beginning to be afraid of Cary,'" quoted Wait slowly. "Did you have any reason ever to doubt the sincerity of Drew's affection for you?"

"I—don't understand."

"Suppose I told you that we found canceled checks among Pett's papers made out to bearer and corresponding exactly to the amounts and dates of the deposits entered in Drew's bankbook. Would that mean anything to you?"

"N-no."

"'Promise results,'" quoted Wait again. "A girl with money—lots of money—is an invitation to fortune hunters. Surely it must have occurred to you. Surely you have wondered about men's sincerity. Please for a moment consider what I am about to say. We know that Pett embezzled—stole from you—a very large sum of money. We know that he tried and failed to replace it. We know that he seems to have supplied Drew with money and that Drew promised results! We know that you always expected simply to turn the care of your fortune over to your husband when you married and that—mistakenly, I think—you were not trained to see to the care of it yourself and thus would have been—were, in fact, very easily deceived. Now then, suppose Drew learned of Pett's defalcation. Suppose he and Pett made up a scheme for their mutual benefit——"

"Not——"

"Yes. Suppose Pett agreed to furnish the money necessary for Drew's—call it courtship. And Drew promised to supply the necessary charm to win you over and make you his wife. Whereupon Drew was to be well supplied with money for the rest of his life. And Pett's embezzlement would never come to light, for Drew would, as Pett would advise you, take over the care of your money with, always, Pett's approval and help. Pett's reasoning would be that this would save him from exposure and that he would see to it that Drew would treat you well—or would try to. Pett's was the type of man who could deceive himself almost as well as he could deceive others. And then——"

"But Marcus didn't try to deceive us. He brought the reports and you said yourself that he had made no effort to hide the shortage."

"He had to bring the reports. He was willing enough to take them away again. However . . ." Wait paused thoughtfully while his fingers traced the carved design on the arm of the gilded french chair in which he sat. "However, I've a curious notion about Pett. I think, odd as it sounds, his conscience got the better of him. I don't know exactly why or how, but it's the only way to explain a kind of vacillation on his part. For instance that telephone call; he denied having made it but we investigated the thing and it certainly was a call from his house and no one else there would be at all likely to telephone to you in the dead of night. Well then, I think that was conscience getting at him," said Wait slowly. "In the dark, cold hours, nagging him to a confession. He must have felt that, as your mother said, you and she would have forgiven him if he confessed his embezzlement and would have refused to prosecute. But when you answered the telephone he lost his courage again and would not answer. And when he came here the night he was murdered I think he came with the intention of telling your mother the truth. But someone stopped him. The logical surmise is that someone believed Pett knew something of Drew's murder. Yes," said Wait. "It's the only way to explain Pett's actions. His scheme to marry you to Drew failed and Drew was subsequently murdered. Perhaps Pett was afraid, too, that someone knew of that scheme and that it was bound to come out sooner or later; he was the type of man, I think, who would make such a plan in a kind of cowardly desperation but would confess to embezzlement rather than run the risk of being mixed up in a murder case."

"Marcus was our friend."

"His own friend first. Once his scheme had worked and

you were safely married to Drew he would be safe. Who, mainly, objected to your marrying Drew?"

"My mother."

"It wasn't Pett then?"

Dorcas did not reply. For all at once in a moment of revelation so clear that it was cruel she saw the truth of Jacob Wait's hypothesis. Saw it so clearly that she cried with trembling lips: "Yes, it's true. I was blind . . ." For she remembered with terrible clearness certain things. Ronald's theatricalisms; her own insistent feeling, even that last night, of being forced to play an unrehearsed role in an unread play. How could she have failed to perceive the falsity of that last desperate scene he had actually staged! Desperate because of her money. She had felt that falsity but had not understood it. Had the attacks on Ronald stiffened her own defense of him and her own will to believe him, or had her self-conceit closed her eyes to his lack of sincerity? Neither perhaps, or both. And it didn't matter, for the thing was done. But . . . She said it aloud: "But who killed Ronald?"

"And killed Marcus. The man who came to the apartment as you struggled with Drew. The man who loved you and wanted to protect you——"

"No—no! No one came."

"Locke came."

"You cannot—you are trying to frighten me. You have no proof——"

"I am as certain that he was there as I shall ever be certain of anything."

"That isn't proof."

"There'll be proof. Nothing—nothing in the world can happen and leave no trace of its happening. Locke came and shot him," said Wait. "And in your heart you know it. I'm sorry, Mrs Locke. It won't be the first time a man has killed another man because he loved a woman."

"Not Jevan—no—no, I tell you, no one came. No one knew I was there. Ronald was alive when I left——"

"Where is Locke?"

"He—I don't know. I don't know where he is. He didn't kill Ronald. He couldn't——"

"I had men watching. If they've let him escape—but we'll find him."

"Not Jevan——"

She must have tried to cling to the detective's arm, for she remembered after she heard the jar of the big door closing that he had thrust her away and then, kindly, had put her in a chair and said nothing. And had gone.

But Jevan hadn't killed Ronald. Jevan couldn't have killed him.

And if he had she still loved him. Loved him and knew, now, that she loved him and would love him as long as her breath came and her pulses beat.

After a while she began to be obsessed with the feeling that she must act. That she must find Jevan; must warn him; must do something to prevent his being caught in the inexorable trap that would be his arrest. She went into the hall and into the library. Her mother and Sophie were not there and Jevan had not returned and it was only chance that she sat down beside the table, trying desperately to discover a course of action and, after a long time, happened to look down at the newspaper below her ringed left hand. And it was open, as Sophie had left it, at the want ads and personals and the word "Elise" leaped at her out of the black forest of print.

Elise. It was a notice in the personal column and it was very short. It said simply: "Elise: Schumanze Court apartment nine Sunday night money. W."

That was all. And she snatched at it instantly, almost frantically. The straw floating toward her. The match touched to that already laid charge which was her need to act.

Elise. Schumanze Court apartment: W must mean Willy, trying as always in his fumbling, inept way to be of help.

He had said Elise over the telephone; he'd been looking for the woman with the green scarf. Nine o'clock.

She was at the door looking at the hall clock, which said a quarter to nine. She must hurry.

In her room she was reminded eerily of another night when she had gone like that, into darkness, tiptoeing down the stairs. She pulled a fur coat over the little bright print dress she wore; snatched a hat—any hat—gloves. This time, as if a cool, prepared voice had reminded her, she took her pocketbook and made sure there was money in it. She might, of course, be stopped by the police the moment she stepped out the door. Reporters might seize upon her. But she was going.

A white, taut face with a crimson mouth and great dark eyes that were frightened looked back at her instantaneously as she adjusted her small fur-trimmed hat. Did women always stop before a mirror, even before such an errand as hers?

No one, again, was in the hall; no one could have heard the little rustle of her skirt as she went down the stairs and across the wide length of the hall and let herself cautiously out the front door.

It was dark and very foggy. She saw no one at all. She waited a moment and listened for voices beyond the halo of light above the doorway, or for a footstep, and heard neither. Cautiously she ventured under the light and was not stopped. She reached the gate and welcome shadows of tall shrubs. She opened the gate carefully and still no one stopped her.

A few minutes later, three blocks away, along what seemed to be otherwise a completely empty street, she saw a taxi and hailed it.

She gave the driver a number that was not Ronald's but was perhaps a half block away.

Nine.

The Chevrolet clock said nine-ten when they reached it. The bridge was up and delayed them and when they turned at last into Schumanze Court ten more minutes must have passed.

She paid and dismissed the driver, waiting until he had gone before she turned toward the apartment house where Ronald had lived. Schumanze Court was deserted; in the distance there might have been a vague figure or two of pedestrians; no one was near at hand. Rows of apartment houses, gleams of light from shaded windows. Lights from entrances, light streaming out thinly from a door she suddenly remembered.

If she could avoid the doorman! She did avoid him. He wasn't in the small foyer and the elevator door was closed. She went quickly inside, then turned up the stairway.

The apartment house was very quiet. She had fled blindly down those very stairs. Afraid not only of Ronald—afraid, too, of the apartment itself, of the mirrors and the white divan and the blank white door. Afraid instinctively of something that—that had not yet happened and that yet had cast ahead of it a kind of foreshadowing.

As if the mirrors had known it was going to happen. As if the very walls had known what they were about to witness and had warned her; had said go, go quickly, go before it is too late.

She reached the hall and there was the door to the apartment. No one was about and there was no sound. The light was dim in the long narrow hall but the whole length of it was visible and she was sure there was no one there.

She listened. There were no voices from the apartment. It was at least twenty minutes after nine.

She was unprepared; she hadn't thought of entering the apartment; she hadn't considered what she was going to do except that she must come. Should she go back to the first floor and ring? But it seemed silly to ring an empty apartment. Besides, the doorman would see her; she couldn't risk it a second time. She had, of course, no key. Stupid of her.

But she had expected someone to be there—Willy and—and this girl. Elise. And Jevan.

Well, what could she do? There was certainly no one anywhere around. There was no sound at all coming from the other side of that neat, white-painted door with RONALD DREW on a card still affixed in a little neat panel upon it.

She put out her hand as if to knock.

And saw what in the semi-dusk of the hall she had not before seen.

The door was open perhaps an inch and the room beyond was dark.

CHAPTER 20

THEY HAD BEEN THERE, then, and had gone. Or they had not come yet and the door had been left open for them when they came. (Who left it open or by what arrangement did not occur to her.) Or they were not coming and the notice in the paper had meant some other Elise; some other apartment; some other concern.

Speculations, none of them very sensible, raced through her mind as she stood there, looking at that black strip. There was still no sound from inside the apartment and the half-formed impulse to knock or even to speak died away. What was beyond the door? An empty apartment of course.

And if they hadn't yet come they would come soon. By "they" she meant Jevan. Jevan and Willy and the mysterious Elise.

She never thought of the plainly prudent course, which was to go away. To go back home and wait until Jevan returned, or Willy. She would probably, in the end, have done that very thing, however, had not the elevator rumbled in the distance and stopped at that floor.

It brought an unexpected end to her isolation. The narrow hall which she remembered with poignant clearness stretched away past other doors (past the door into the kitchen of Ronald's apartment, among others) to a dim red light indicating a fire escape at its other end. Midway it was bisected by a wider corridor upon which the elevator opened. Thus the elevator door was not visible from where she stood but she could hear it; could hear it stop and the door as it slid open, and the voices of people.

They mustn't see her there. Her picture was in all the papers; they would recognize her immediately.

The voices came nearer, laughing; there were several people. The instant before they reached the intersection of the corridors Dorcas pushed the door of the apartment further open and stepped into the darkness beyond.

It was altogether dark with only a small path of light coming from the open door and falling dimly on the carpet and a corner of a white divan. There was not a sound in the apartment and the voices in the corridor outside seemed to be receding. She waited.

Still no sound. Certainly the apartment was empty. But the door was open and it was by this time considerably after nine.

Somewhere near the door there must be the electric light switch; Ronald's hand had reached behind her and pressed it. She fumbled into the darkness beside the door. She could not find the switch for a moment and in that moment the room around her became strangely sentient, reminding her insistently of the other time she had stood at that door. She had a quick, queer consciousness of, particularly, the mirrors, watching from the darkness around her and adding a new chapter to their silent record. Then she found the little button and pulled it downward and it clicked and there was no light.

No light. But naturally it had been turned off; they always cut off light and gas in an empty apartment. Probably the apartment would be empty for some time; until what had happened there was forgotten.

Ought she to go and try otherwise to find Jevan? Or ought she to wait? Wait and remember Ronald's flushed face and bright eyes, eyes that looked over her shoulder as if someone were there and when she had turned there was no one. Only a white door that seemed just to quiver into place. "You can't go. I won't let you go. . . . The old melodramas from which I have so lavishly borrowed . . . darling. . . ."

She mustn't let herself remember. Just beside her was the white divan; in the darkness a little away was the table which had held the white table lamp. And the telephone. Beside the table Ronald had fallen.

The voices from the corridor had completely died away.

The time during which she stood there in the darkness, undecided, assailed by things the room itself seemed to seek to remind her of, could have been actually only a moment or two, although it seemed much longer. The door had of its own volition swung slowly back to its original position, so now the band of faint light from the hall was only an inch or two in width. And except for the ugly memories which surrounded her as the darkness surrounded her, so Ronald's face swam out of it, Ronald's face and Ronald's words, she had not a sense of danger. Instead it seemed safe. Safe and deserted, except for the mirrors, and if anyone approached by way of the stairway she would know it.

She must have decided to wait, for she turned to grope for the white divan and it was just as her fingers touched the rough fabric that she realized someone else was in the room.

She never knew exactly how she knew it unless it was by the barely perceptible little sound of suction as if a door somewhere opened. But she did know it and she knew that the door that opened so gently but unmistakably was either the door leading to the kitchen or the bedroom door.

Her fingers froze on the divan. There was no sound—or was there the barely audible sound of light footsteps across the room? She could see nothing in that suffocating blackness, could hear nothing except—except all at once, breaking out into that silence in queer jumbled rush, there was a voice. Two voices, indistinguishable and muffled, and then, blind-

ing, bewildering, terribly loud and yet muffled, the sound of
a revolver shot.

It was a quick, reverberating shock of sound, mingled suddenly with other sounds, footsteps running, a door banging
somewhere and another door, a rush of motion in the blackness of the room and more footsteps running lightly somewhere near her.

She must have tried to reach the door beside her and escape that fated apartment, for all at once she found herself
clutching into the darkness for the door, suddenly and
sharply aware of someone very near her and then, before she
could stop herself, her hands encountered the rough material
of a coat which bumped squarely into her. Arms fumbled
and flung themselves around her and—and it was Jevan. She
knew it was Jevan. His close embrace, his nearness, that intangible, primitive something that makes recognition told her
it was Jevan.

And he must have known her by the same elemental
sense, for he was sharply still for an instant and then his arms
held her closer and he cried huskily: "Dorcas! You here!"

She clung to him. There were retreating sounds somewhere
—or were there? It was all at once very quiet.

"Good God, Dorcas——"

His face was against her own. "Dorcas, what are you doing here?"

"I came—oh, Jevan, what was it—the shot——"

"Don't tremble like that. It's all right. I'll see to things. I'll
—wait, Dorcas, let me shut that door. If anyone heard——"

His arms left her. In the immense silence that followed
that momentary confusion and chaos of sound she could hear
him move to the door and close it very softly, shutting out
that crack of light, and she heard him move back toward her
through the complete darkness. His hands reached for her
and he whispered: "Dorcas, you've got to get out of here.
I'll help you. You know—that. Where's the revolver?"

"Revolver?"

"Yes, I——" He stopped. His arms were around her again,
holding her close to him. He said all at once, clearly in the
silence, "I've got matches. Wait, Dorcas."

Again his arms relinquished her. She could hear him search
in his pockets and then there was the sputter of a match. It
didn't light the room; it made only a small and flickering

glow as he held it and looked at her and around him and turned abruptly toward the open bedroom door.

She followed him. Just at the bedroom door a small hidden draft struck the little flame and it wavered once and went out.

Jevan swore and struck another.

It flared and he went into the bedroom and stopped almost on the threshold. She saw him moisten his lips. She saw the flame jerk and steady itself in his hands. She heard him mutter something that sounded like, "Don't look," but it was too late.

For she, too, now could see it. Flung down like so much rubbish, something used and thrown away, a woman lay huddled between the two beds. Blond hair was disheveled under a small green hat which was crushed under her head. A checked sport coat had fallen apart, showing a shabby black crepe dress. Little high-heeled pumps, one of them turned fantastically as she had fallen, had thin soles and scuffed toes. And that match burned down to Jevan's fingers and went out, making a tiny red spark in the blackness.

"It's Elise," said Jevan. "It's Elise."

He must have lighted another match. Dorcas clung to a chair and watched the little light moving around as if Jevan were looking for something. A candle of course. He found it, however, in the living room and lighted it and it made a larger, clearer flame and was an ornamental white candle, huge and heavily dipped in gold and added a nightmare note to the thing. For the flame was picked up by the watchful mirrors and reflected a hundred times and the shadowy silhouettes of their figures were reflected, too, eerily, so they filled the room.

Then the flame moved toward the bedroom and vanished and left the mirrors blank again.

Jevan was kneeling, holding the candle with one hand, like a solitary vigil light above the dead girl.

"Is she . . . ?" began Dorcas and Jevan said he didn't know. He said he couldn't tell. He held the candle over Elise's crumpled, tragic little body and said there was blood on her dress and he couldn't tell whether she was alive or dead and he'd get a doctor.

And he got up again from where he'd been kneeling in

that crowded space between the two white, couchlike beds
and came to Dorcas.

"You've got to get out first," he said. "Understand, Dorcas. I think she's still alive; at least there's a chance. So I'm
going to get a doctor here. And you must leave."

"But——"

"Oh, my darling," cried Jevan suddenly. "When I found
you here I thought you'd killed her and I——" His voice
broke. The candlelight made his face look very white and
masklike. He said: "But you didn't. I know you didn't. So
I've got to—what's the matter, Dorcas? Why are you looking
so strangely at me? Why——"

"But I thought—I heard the shot and then you came and I
thought—for a moment—just an instant, Jevan, I thought
you—but I wasn't afraid. But now I know it wasn't you."

There was a small, clear silence. Then Jevan said jerkily:
"Faith. Blind, instinctive faith. Queer. . . . I know you
didn't fire the shot. And you're willing to believe that I—
all right, Dorcas. We'll stand together. Except I'm going to
make you leave now. Before the doctor comes. I'll call him.
There's a chance of saving her. And I'm going to call the
police. As soon as you——"

Jevan turned toward the telephone. He was saying something about getting the doctor first. "Then we'll find a way
to get you out of here before he comes," said Jevan and put
his hand on the telephone; exactly as he did so it rang.
The sharp shrill of it was horribly loud and demanding.
Jevan jerked his hand away as if the thing had been electri-
cally charged and his eyes darted around the apartment and
fastened on the door that led to the kitchen and he cried:
"I'm a fool. Wait, Dorcas. Don't touch the telephone." He
ran, leaving the candle on the table, to the door, pulled it
open and disappeared. The telephone rang again and behind
her, in the darkness of the bedroom, a girl with bright blond
hair and a checked coat lay with blood on her dress and
staining the floor.

Who? Not Jevan—not Jevan. But who then?

Jevan was back, running, face emerging into the faint light
from the candle.

"There's nobody in the kitchen." He flung an empty book
of matches upon the table. "I was a fool not to look sooner.
There's been plenty of time for him to get away. I didn't

realize . . ." The telephone shrilled again and he took it and said: "Hello . . . hello . . ."

"Don't answer," cried Dorcas. "Don't——"

"It's the police," whispered Jevan. "It's Wait." And spoke into the telephone. "Yes, I'm here. And, Wait, get a doctor, will you? Hurry. All right. I'll stay here. But listen—listen to me. There's a dead girl here. At least . . . Yes, I know. But whoever killed her has just escaped. I don't know who . . . All right. All right."

He put down the telephone. A queer flash of something like admiration went over his face. "What a man," he said and turned swiftly to Dorcas. "But he's not to find you here. Come on, Dorcas. There's a way out. Down the hall there's a service door. It's just opposite the elevator. You'll have to be careful. Watch the elevator. For God's sake, hurry——"

"I'm not going."

"Have you left anything—gloves, bag—where——"

"Jevan, I'm not going."

This time he heard her and jerked around toward her, his face jutting out in sharp relief above the candle flame.

"What do you mean?"

"I'm going to stay. With you. I didn't shoot her and you didn't and we——"

He didn't stop to convince her. He simply took her up in his arms, sweeping her off the floor, and carried her to the door leading to the kitchen. There was no use struggling against him.

"You've got to go. You're a little fool if you don't. I can't carry you. You've got to . . ." They were in the kitchen and the door was open and a flashlight streamed fully upon them. Beyond the blinding light Wait's voice said in a leisurely way:

"Don't go."

Jevan stopped and let Dorcas slide downward till she stood beside him.

"You——"

"I was downstairs. Somebody's getting a doctor. Don't go, Mrs Locke. Where's the girl?"

Wait was not alone; two plain-clothes men and two policemen crowded into the kitchen and with them Sophie. Sophie, neat and trim in her black coat with the silver fox collar and small black hat and pearl earrings, but she was frightened and pale and put her arm around Dorcas.

"Good God, Dorcas, why did you come here? I saw you. I had to follow you. Wait was already here; I couldn't warn you. He saw me on the street and made me tell him why I came. But he already knew you were here; a policeman followed you from the house. Oh, my dear, you shouldn't have come. What's happened? They said somebody was hurt. What——"

"In here, please," said someone. They followed the policeman back into the white, mirrored living room. The men were crowding at the bedroom door. They were talking and phrases came to Dorcas' and Sophie's ears.

"She's dead all right."

"Maybe not. Let me hold a mirror to her lips."

"That's right. Take this——"

"Easy now."

And Wait's voice, clear: "Who is she?"

Jevan did not reply; there were other voices and then Wait's again: "Get lights. They're likely cut off. O'Brien. Phone down and tell the janitor to turn 'em on again. Hones, get out there at the door. Now then, Locke, who is this girl? Is she the one that came to the house and——"

"It's Elise," said Jevan.

"Elise. Elise who? Why did you shoot her?"

"I didn't shoot her."

The man O'Brien was shouting into the telephone and words from the bedroom were lost. Sophie and Dorcas, clutching each other's hands, stood there listening. And O'Brien put down the telephone and began snapping lamps off and on as if doing so would hasten the electric current's being turned on and the sputter of the matches the men were recklessly lighting died away and Wait came out of the bedroom carrying the solitary candle, and one of the policemen emerged in his wake with the flashlight.

The candle and the flashlight vied with each other, and the mirrors were crowded now with black silhouettes and Wait's eyes shone and glistened above the candle's flame.

"You'll have to come clean, Locke," he said. "I've got you." His dark eyes swept around the room and singled out Dorcas for a second and he said to Jevan, "You can still keep your wife out of it. If you'll confess——"

"No, no, Jevan," cried Dorcas on a great surge of terror. "You mustn't. You——"

"Hush, Dorcas," said Jevan quietly. "I'll tell the truth, Wait. That woman in there is the woman who came to the house. The woman we've been trying to find. You see, she was Drew's wife. Elise——"

"Drew's wife? He wasn't married. We'd have found the record."

"Oh yes," said Jevan. "He was married. Nobody knew it; he was married in another county and the record is there; they kept it a secret, or rather he did, and they didn't get along and separated but not legally. And Elise——" He stopped and said: "Do you think she'll live?"

"I don't know. The doctor will be here in a few minutes," said Wait and Sophie stirred and said: "Can I do anything for her?"

"Thank you. There's nothing we can do. We don't dare move her until the doctor comes. The best thing for her is to wait." Sophie sat down on the white divan beside Dorcas and Wait looked at Jevan. "Exactly what was Elise's part in this? Did she know that Drew wanted to marry Mrs Locke?"

"I don't know," said Jevan. "I know only that Elise came to the house and that she was his wife. She must have known something or she couldn't have come to see Mrs Locke. We— that is, naturally I assumed that she wanted something from my wife. And I naturally wanted to find her again—to discover what, if anything, she knew—mainly to keep her from coming again to my wife——"

"Blackmail?"

"Well, yes, I thought of it. I didn't want my wife to be annoyed or worried by her. I didn't really want my wife to know of the girl's existence. And I thought—well, at first I thought either that Elise herself had killed Drew or that she had some evidence she was willing to sell. I wasn't, of course, absolutely sure she was Drew's wife but Bench's description of the woman in the checked coat seemed to fit what I knew of her. And then after she'd gone—or we supposed she'd gone—I came upon a scarf. A green silk scarf; it was there at home—in the Whipple house, I mean, near the stairway. Looked as if she'd dropped it. To me, then, it was a tangible proof of the—well, the threat her visit contained. That, of course, was in the afternoon before Marcus was killed."

"Yes."

"As you know, I phoned Willy and we met and talked and

then came back to the house. And when we got there the police were there and Marcus' body had been found. So then I thought that Elise must have done it."

"Why?"

"Because she'd been there and nobody saw her leave. Because conceivably Marcus could have known that she murdered Drew——"

"Murdered Drew! Do you know that she——"

"No, no. I don't know that she murdered Drew. But I thought so then. Jealousy, a quarrel—oh, there were a hundred motives she could have had for killing him. Thus if Marcus knew of it or even if she thought he knew it, she would have had a motive for killing Marcus."

"And why didn't you tell me of Elise and Drew's marriage?"

Jevan hesitated. Inside the bedroom a policeman murmured something to another policeman of which the word "minutes" alone was distinguishable.

"Because," said Jevan. "I wanted to find Elise myself and question her."

"That won't do, Locke. The truth is that you did not want me to know of her existence until you had what you considered proof of her guilt. And the reason you didn't want me to know of her was because you realized that she provided the strongest possible motive for your wife to have murdered Drew. The other woman, the wife with prior claim, the wife whose existence and claims Drew had kept a secret until he had sufficiently entangled your wife——"

"My wife was not 'entangled.' And my wife knew nothing of this girl, Elise."

"But you did. And you met her here tonight. Why? Because she was to provide an out for you. Because you intended to arrange what would appear to be a suicide—a suicide that would also look like a confession. Perhaps you even intended to write a little suicide note, confessing to the murders and signed Elise. Did you?"

"No! That's not true!" began Jevan furiously and checked himself and said more quietly: "I planned nothing of the kind. I didn't shoot her. I have no revolver, I——"

"You could have disposed of it."

"There's no revolver in the apartment, Mr Wait," said the policeman he had called O'Brien.

"I didn't expect there would be. When the men come from headquarters have two of them make a complete search."

"Yes sir."

"How long, Locke, have you known of Elise and how did you know? You say that you had never seen her before."

"That's true. Someone told me of her. I've known it for —some time."

"If you knew Drew was already married why didn't you tell your wife—before she was your wife, that is?"

"I didn't—want to."

"You'd have preferred seeing her illegally married to him?"

"She didn't marry him."

"She might have done so. Why didn't you tell her?"

"Reasons," said Jevan crisply. "Perhaps I wanted her consent to our marriage on—on another basis."

Wait shook his head impatiently. And someone at the door said quickly: "Here's the doctor."

Lights flashed suddenly on as the doctor arrived. Their brightness was bewildering, as if the room and all it held were plunged suddenly into a different dimension.

Dorcas blinked and took a long breath; she was sitting on the white divan beside Sophie. She caught a distant reflection of herself in a mirror opposite. A girl with an utterly stiff, blank white face and Dorcas' hat.

The doctor, a big man, glanced curiously at the two women on the divan and tramped heavily into the bedroom. Wait followed him. Jevan, looking very pale and tense, came to Dorcas.

"We'll get a good lawyer," he said and Sophie put her black-gloved hand over Dorcas' hand.

"Exactly what *did* happen?" she asked Jevan, whispering. "Why did you and Dorcas come here?"

He could not tell her. A stretcher was being maneuvered through the bedroom door. Jevan stood in front of Dorcas so she could see only his broad, tweed-colored shoulders.

"But she's alive," he told her as the dismal little procession vanished. "She's alive and has a chance."

"A small chance," said Wait at his side again. "So small— why did you shoot her, Locke? There's no one else who could have done it unless it was your wife. You were both here. Which one of you shot her?"

"She didn't shoot Elise," said Jevan. "And I didn't."

Wait looked at him quietly for a moment. Then he went to the table, pulled up a small white chair and sat down. The mirrors set in dull blue walls reflected his face and the back of his glossy head a hundred times so there were a hundred Waits in the room. Wait said: "I'm arresting you now, Locke, and charging you with the murder of Drew and of Pett and with the attempted murder of that girl. Your wife told us the whole story of the night Drew was killed. She—had to do it," said Wait with a gleam of humanity. "There was an instrument of persuasion that came to my hand and I was obliged to use it. I mean," he explained, "a note which, coupled with some other evidence, led me to believe that Pett and Drew were partners in a scheme by which Drew was to marry Mrs Locke." Dorcas listened while he explained carefully, fully, with irresistible truth.

Sophie listened, too, and cried: "Marcus! And we never dreamed—oh, Dorcas, it must be true. Marcus always rather favored Ronald, remember? It must be true. Did Jevan know? Is that why he——" She caught herself sharply with a frightened glance at Wait, who did not appear to have heard it, for he went on: "The night he was killed Drew made a last desperate effort to induce your wife to elope with him. He grew frantic as she resisted him and tried to force her to marry him by any means that occurred to him. He didn't want her simply to elope with him, he wanted to marry her. Elise . . ." Wait paused for a second. "Elise presents a new angle. I think she must have known of his plans; perhaps he promised her money when he succeeded. In that case she might have had a fairly substantial nuisance value. Elise——" He frowned, shrugged a little and said: "I'm inclined to think, however, that Elise was only incidental, quite aside from the main issue. Perhaps she did come to your wife for money, perhaps not. If she lives we'll know. Certainly there was a reason for silencing her; thus, certainly, she knows something. But as I see it, that is her only importance. And what she knows may be of no real importance to me. The guilty flee," said Wait rather sententiously, "where a shadow pursues." He paused a thoughtful moment which appeared to confirm his belief, for he went on: "At any rate you killed Drew. Your wife has told me everything——"

"Oh no, no," cried Dorcas. "I didn't tell——" And put both hands across her mouth. How could she let him know that they still had no proof of his presence? Jevan didn't

look at her. She started toward him and Sophie put her
hand on her arm and stopped her and Jevan said steadily:
"Very well then. If she's told you everything you know that
Drew was alive when she left his apartment."

"When did you kill him?"

"I didn't kill him."

"Then your wife did and you are trying to protect her.
Oh, Locke, don't you see that it's either you or your wife?
Don't you——"

"Don't say anything, Jevan. Don't——"

"Hush, Dorcas," whispered Sophie. "Be still. Jevan will
see a way."

But Jevan didn't. He put up his chin and looked squarely
at the detective and said: "Yes, I see that. I knew it would
come sometime. Well, it wasn't my wife."

"Is that a confession?"

"It's nothing of the kind." Jevan's eyes flickered toward
one of the plain-clothes men and for the first time Dorcas
was aware that the plain-clothes man had a shorthand tablet
in his hand and was writing. Every word of it, then, was going on that inexorable record. To be quoted later—at the
trial. Her heart turned over inside her. She must stop Jevan.
And she couldn't, for he said: "Yes, I was here. After my
wife had gone."

"Was Drew alive?"

Jevan's mouth was tight and white. He said: "I refuse to
answer. I must have a lawyer."

"You mean he was dead and your wife had shot him and
you knew it?"

"No," said Jevan. "My wife did not kill him."

"Then you did. You killed him and then killed Pett because he knew, somehow, what you had done. And then you
decoyed this girl here and shot her."

"I didn't shoot her."

"Then it was your wife."

"No."

"Mrs Locke, why did you come here tonight? You were
followed, you know, from your house and you went out of
your way to give the wrong address to the taxi driver who
brought you here. My man followed you and let me know
you were here and I guessed you had come to meet and warn
your husband. But I didn't guess you were—one of you or
both of you—going to do murder."

"Don't say anything, Dorcas; you aren't obliged to talk," said Jevan swiftly but Dorcas cried: "No, no. Jevan was here, too, but it was the personal notice—Elise and Schumanze Court and——"

"What do you mean?"

"The notice in the personal column," repeated Dorcas and told him.

" 'W,' " said Wait. "That means what?"

"Willy put it in," said Jevan. "He was trying to help. He knows nothing about this except that I wanted to find Elise. So he thought he'd help and put that notice in the paper and told me of it after he had done so. So of course I came in the hope that it might, after all, bring Elise here. It's nothing to Willy; he's out of this entirely. I got here and came up to the apartment and it was unlocked. I came in the kitchen door and it was dark and—and no one seemed to be about. You don't have to believe this, of course, but it's true and I'm telling you exactly what happened."

"Go on."

"Well—then I came into this room. It was dark; the lights were cut off, as you know. I had tried them in the kitchen. It was perfectly still and I thought no one was here. Then all at once I heard a voice. I couldn't tell what it was, for it was just a jumble of words, but it seemed to come from the bedroom and then all at once without any more warning than that there was a shot. Then I—I'm not sure what happened, for it was so dark, but I do know that there was the sound of somebody running and of a door banging——"

"Was Mrs Locke in the room?"

"Yes," said Dorcas. "He—Jevan had just come into the room from the kitchen. I heard the door——"

"But it was dark, you say. You couldn't be sure——"

"I am sure," said Dorcas. "For right after the shot we—we bumped into each other in the darkness."

"After he left the bedroom, you mean?"

"It was someone else in the bedroom," said Jevan. "My wife was over there near the door. She couldn't have escaped from the bedroom and got there before I found her."

"But you are trying to make me believe that somebody shot Elise, escaped through this room in the dark——"

"And out the kitchen way. That's exactly what happened," said Jevan.

Wait shook his head again and looked at Jevan with a hint of something that was almost admiration in his eyes.

"A good story," he said. "But who did it if you didn't? Who had the motive? Who had the opportunity? Confess, Locke."

Again there was a little electric silence while the two men measured one another and walls and mirrors, watching them, knew a thing they could not tell.

Then Wait said slowly, almost musically: "Why did you come to find Elise if you had no thought of killing her?"

"I wanted to find out what she knew. To buy her off if I had to. To——"

Wait's eyes flashed. A gust of impatience went over him; his eyes shone and he leaned forward and said: "I repeat that you came to silence her in another way. And you've done it—unless in spite of everything she lives. You murdered Drew and Pett and——"

There was a commotion in the doorway; two policemen grasping at either side someone who came reluctantly and sputtered at every step and was Willy. He went dead white when he saw Dorcas and Jevan and Sophie. He said, or tried to say: "It's an outrage. An outrage. I've done nothing——"

"I found him over on Cuahanan Street. He was starting his car and it's been parked there for some time. He was trying to get away and resisted us. We thought we'd better bring him along——"

"That's right," said Wait. "All right, Devany. What's your story?"

CHAPTER 21

WILLY RUBBED his forehead and sat limply in a great white chair into which the policemen thrust him and said rather dazedly a number of times that he hadn't any story. He wound up giving Jevan a pleading look and saying: "What's happened? They said somebody's been shot. You—you didn't kill her, did you, Jevan?"

"Kill who?" demanded Wait sharply.

"Why, Elise, of course. I oughtn't to have put the notice in the paper," gibbered Willy. "But I thought it was a good idea. It seemed like it at the time. Good God, what are we going to do now? Is she really dead?"

"Don't talk, Willy," said Jevan. "You're out of this and I've told them so. I didn't kill her of course. Or Dorcas——"

"Dorcas," cried Willy wildly. "Was she here too?"

"Willy, listen," said Jevan desperately. "Don't answer any questions. Don't say anything. And get yourself a lawyer. I'm going to. I've got to."

"Yes," said Wait dryly. "He's under a murder charge," and watched Willy, who went from white to a sort of pea green.

"But he——"

"Shut up!" snapped Jevan. "It's not your fight."

"Is Elise dead?" asked Willy, paying no attention at all to Jevan and turning to Wait.

"She's barely alive. There's a chance. That's all. You knew she was Drew's wife."

"Willy," cried Jevan and still Willy wouldn't listen.

"Yes, of course. I was the one that told Jevan. I learned it only accidentally."

"How?" said Wait. It brought Willy up shortly and he gave Wait a harassed look and said:

"Friend of hers and mine. Girl named Dolly White. Dances in a night club with Elise. Anyway, she told me and as Dorcas was already engaged to be married to Jevan and Ronald was apparently out of the picture I didn't see any use in spreading it. Drew's own business. But all the same he was a dirty skunk, you know. Trying to marry Dorcas without divorcing his real wife. Elise wouldn't divorce him; wanted money, I suppose. Well, anyway, I guess that's all," said Willy.

"So you told Locke that Drew was already married?"

"Huh?" said Willy in a startled way. "Oh. Oh yes, I told him. Had to. Drew was still after Dorcas; wouldn't give her up."

"Yes, I know," said Wait. "He induced her to come to this apartment with him the night before her wedding. She has admitted that," he said as Willy jerked anxiously around to look at Dorcas. "She's admitted her presence here, so you may as well go on. You knew she was here that night?"

"I—no, no, of course not."

"You saw her? Tell the truth, Devany."

"No. I mean I——"

"You knew she was here and that's why you went to find Locke? Isn't that right?"

"No, no. Certainly not."

"Oh, go ahead, Willy, if you must," said Jevan. "I told you not to talk. I wanted to keep you out of it. But now you've told this much you'll have to go on." He turned to Wait. "Yes, he knew it. He drove past the Whipple house and saw my—my wife meet Drew and followed them to the apartment and then tried to find me. But my wife was gone before Drew was killed. I'll swear it."

"That right, Devany?"

"I—yes," said Willy miserably. "You see, I knew what a skunk Drew was. And the wedding was next day—and if he got Dorcas to elope with him it'd be an awful mess for Dorcas. Somebody had to do something. I couldn't, so I went to get Jevan and finally found him and——" He stopped abruptly with an expression of absolute horror on his face.

"And you brought Locke here," finished Wait. "That right, Devany?"

"No, no," cried Willy.

"You brought Locke here. You waited for him while he came up here to this apartment——"

"No, no," cried Willy again, the force of his denial making it like an admission.

Jevan stirred and said abruptly: "It's all right, Willy. He knows. . . . All right, Wait, you've won. Willy did find me and tell me Dorcas was here. Told me Dorcas was married and that he was afraid Drew was—well, it's as he said. He knew what a skunk Drew was; guessed he had some scheme and knew, knowing Drew, it was crooked. Willy knew, too, that it was up to me to come. My fight——"

"That's what you said, Jevan. I wanted to come up here too."

"But he didn't come. He waited in the car for me. I came up alone."

"And found Drew already dead," cried Willy. "Drew was already dead when he got here, so he couldn't have——"

"Willy," shouted Jevan. "For God's sake, shut up! Drew was alive!"

Still Willy didn't see, for he looked at Jevan and at Wait and cried: "Drew was dead. Jevan told me he was dead when he got here. And he rubbed off fingerprints and——"

"*Willy!*" It was Jevan again. And Willy turned a puzzled face toward him and said: "I don't see why you're not telling the truth. You didn't kill him. He was dead when you got here." And his feverish blue eyes went to Dorcas. Went to Dorcas and fastened upon her and widened in anguish as he saw what he had done.

"Dorcas—Dorcas——"

"Never mind, Willy."

"Dorcas——"

"She didn't kill him. She——"

"Stop. All of you." It was Wait, cutting off Willy's shame and anguish and Jevan's protestations. He turned to Jevan. "So Drew was dead when you arrived. And it was you that wiped those glasses clean of fingerprints and arranged the gun to look like suicide and you did it because you knew Mrs Locke had killed him."

"My wife did not murder Drew," said Jevan. "But I'm going to do something, Wait, that may be wrong. I don't know. I may be making a mistake that can't——" He stopped and then went on rather savagely. "If I'm wrong there's always one thing I can do to right it. See here, Wait, I'll make a trade with you. You send these policemen out of the room and I'll tell you everything I know."

"But you don't want it to go on record and you don't want a police witness. That it, Locke?"

"That's it," said Jevan.

"Jevan, don't be a fool," began Willy and Sophie gave him a look and said: "Do be still, Willy. You've said quite enough."

Wait was looking thoughtfully at Jevan. Small ruby lights were in his dark eyes and his fine small hand tapped the table before him.

Jevan said: "You can't lose by it. I can. But I'm doing you the credit of believing two things. One is that you're above framing any one of us. The other is that you want the truth and only the truth."

The truth. Dorcas did not know why she felt it and there was not time to dig into her mind and analyze it but she knew suddenly that she did not want the truth. She only wanted Wait to let them go, to free Jevan, to call the case closed. But the truth was—was dangerous. She felt the danger and she tried to tell Jevan not to do whatever he was going to do and it was too late. For Wait said suddenly;

"All right, Locke. It's a gamble but I'll take it. You are protected, for my word would not hold against all four of you—at least I'd have a hard time proving that you were all lying. In the event," said Wait rather dryly, "that you're going to tell me who murdered Drew and murdered Pett——"

"You mean," said Jevan grimly, "that if I tell you the truth you'll take what I tell you and use it as you see fit. I know that. I realize it perfectly. But I still think it's worth the chance——"

"Jevan, don't do anything you'll regret," warned Sophie. "But I think, too, that if the detective knows the truth it'll be best for us all. I think you'd better tell him everything. It's reached a place where—where you've got to. Even if——"

She stopped. Dorcas' feeling of apprehension leaped up sharper. "What do you mean, Sophie? Is there anything . . . ?" She wouldn't return Dorcas' look and Wait said abruptly: "All right. You men can all wait outside. In the corridor. Close the door. But watch both doors. Don't let anyone leave and—don't let anyone enter."

Dorcas put her hand on Sophie's and made her look at her. "Sophie, what do you mean? You can't mean——"

Sophie still wouldn't look at her. She whispered: "Hush, Dorcas. I don't mean anything except what I said."

And as the blue-uniformed little exodus completed its filing out the door O'Brien, the last one to go, turned back toward Wait. The very set of his blue shoulders expressed disapproval.

"Any other orders, sir?"

"Don't let anyone leave," repeated Wait. But there was something subtly significant in his dark eyes and O'Brien's disapproval changed all at once to approval.

"Oh," he said. "Sure. Okay, sir." He closed the door. Wait said: "Better sit down, Locke."

Willy, in a great white chair, wriggled uncomfortably and watched Wait. Sophie, erect beside Dorcas on the white divan, reached over to clasp Dorcas' hand and also watched Wait. Jevan sat down and took out a cigarette. He lighted it slowly while the mirrors watched them all. Just over his shoulder was the dead white door which had moved—or had it?—that other night when Dorcas had sat on that same white divan. Jevan looked at Dorcas suddenly over the smoke and said quietly: "Dorcas, if what I'm going to do is wrong, remember I can always undo it." He did not wait for her reply but turned directly to Wait. "All right, Wait. As I said, you've won. Drew was dead when I reached this apartment. I did wipe off fingerprints and try to make the thing look like a suicide. That's true. But it was only because I knew my wife had been here and naturally I wanted to keep her out of the thing if it was at all possible. I did not do it because I thought she'd murdered him. Understand that. And understand, too, that I realize that this admission I'm making could have any number of implications. The chief and most dangerous is—is that if you believe me you are almost bound to believe that my wife killed him. And that I—I appear to be trying, since you've actually arrested me and charged me with murder——"

"I have," agreed Wait.

"I appear to be trying to shift the guilt from myself to my —my wife," said Jevan. "But my wife did not kill Drew. And if you arrest her and charge her with murder I shall immediately confess to doing it myself. It's the only thing I can do and I will, so there's no use in your arresting her."

Wait's eyes and face were completely unfathomable. Jevan, too, was so still he might have been carved in rock; only the white line around his mouth and his desperately watchful eyes gave any evidence of his realization of the grim chance he was taking and making Dorcas take. She thought fleetingly, strangely, of the policemen outside who would not let anyone leave. They were caught, then, like rats in a trap and by Jevan's own confession.

Wait said, his words dropping into that silence like stones: "Is that all?"

"That's all. Isn't it enough?"

"It has its importance. Oh yes——"

"All I ask you to do is to consider what might have happened if my wife did not kill Drew. I know she didn't——"

"How do you know? You keep saying that but how——"

"I know," said Jevan. "Listen—he was alive when she left this room at about nine o'clock. He was dead when I got here about nine-thirty. There's a half an hour to be accounted for. Won't you be fair? Won't you consider——"

Wait moved restlessly. "Very well," he said shortly. "Half an hour. If you didn't kill him and your wife didn't, who was the murderer? Do you know that?"

"I know," said Jevan slowly, "that someone was in the

kitchen of the apartment. My wife said that door over there moved. There were noises in the kitchen which at the time she attributed to sounds Drew made when he opened the refrig——"

"I know all that," said Wait. "She told me. But there was nothing definite. She didn't see anyone. Drew didn't say anyone was there——"

"I say there was somebody there. I don't know who. It might have been Marcus, come to see whether or not Drew's last attempt to marry Dorcas was successful. Impatient of the outcome. Waiting and listening and hoping for Drew's success."

"Marcus Pett was murdered."

"I know. So probably he didn't kill Drew. But someone was there."

"You mean someone was here in the apartment waiting and hiding in the kitchen. Here when Drew and Mrs Locke arrived. Here with Drew's knowledge?"

"That or had a key to the kitchen door and came into the kitchen while Drew and Dorcas were in here. Drew then went to the kitchen and Dorcas heard what she thought was whispering——"

"Elise," said Sophie. "She would have a key."

"Possibly," said Wait. "I'll have that checked. But it would prove nothing. Suppose she was here?"

"And suppose they quarreled," said Jevan. "She and Drew, after Dorcas ran away. Suppose they quarreled because Elise was jealous or—which is as logical—because she was disappointed in his failure to persuade my wife, thus losing the money which could have made them both comfortable all their lives."

Wait shook his head. "Not a strong enough motive. She might be jealous, yes; but there was no need for jealousy, since Mrs Locke refused Drew. She might have been disappointed but she wouldn't have killed him from sheer disappointment. A murder," said Wait, "is almost always done to remove an obstacle—an insupportable obstacle—to something somebody wants. An obstacle that can be removed no other way——"

"Most murders," said Jevan, fighting for his life and for Dorcas'. "Most murders, but what about rage? Suppose she'd been drinking, there in the kitchen."

A spark of light came into Wait's eyes. "There was a glass," he said. "And a cigarette. Mrs Locke, I've asked this before. I repeat: Were you at any time in the kitchen of this apartment?"

"No," said Dorcas out of a nightmare and was dimly surprised to her her own voice speaking. And Jevan said quickly, seizing upon it: "You see, there's proof someone was in the kitchen."

"What exactly did you do when you arrived here, Locke?"

Jevan leaned tensely forward; a falling man clutching at a rope. "I knocked and no one answered. I suppose I knocked several times; there was no sound and I tried the door. It opened and there was a light and I looked in and saw—saw Drew. Over there beside the table. I didn't think he was dead. Not then. I came into the room and shut the door and —and looked at him and realized he was dead and had been shot."

"Where was the revolver?"

"Over there. On the floor beside the divan."

"Out of his reach?"

"Altogether. I—I did think—that is, I——"

"You knew your wife had just gone, so you——"

"I saw three cigarette ends in an ash tray and they had red smudges like lipstick around them. I took those and later, on my way home, threw them out the car window. I saw two glasses and thought they might have been drinking and as I didn't know which one Dorcas might have touched I wiped them both. I wiped the revolver and put it beside him and——"

"And tried to put his fingerprints on it. Yes, I know. And you wiped the telephone and the doorknob and went away."

"Yes."

"Did you go into the kitchen?"

"No."

"Where was Devany all this time?"

"Waiting for me. In his car. Downstairs——"

"You tell me, Devany," cut in Wait. "You say you followed Mrs Locke and Drew here. Then you went to find Locke. You went——"

Willy's thin hands twisted together. "I went to his house and he wasn't there. I didn't know what to do. I drove around and stopped at a drugstore and tried to telephone Drew's apartment. I thought maybe I could get Dorcas on the telephone and could—could tell her to come away—could tell her about Elise—could do something. But no one answered. Then I went to the club and—you know the rest."

"What did Locke mean by telling you it was his fight—when he left you in the car while he came up here?"

"I—don't know," stammered Willy and Sophie gave him an impatient look and said swiftly: "Only an expression of course. And as to that I wouldn't blame Jevan if he did kill Ronald. A man's got a right to protect his own—that is, he would have had a right to, except that, of course, he didn't kill him."

However well she meant it, it pointed to the weakness of their position. Any jury, hearing it, perhaps sympathizing secretly with Jevan, would nevertheless be forced to accede to his guilt. Dorcas saw it with cruel clearness and Wait said abruptly:

"Well, Devany, what then? What did you do?"

"Waited, of course," said Willy, twisting his hands, and looked very worried. "It was about twenty minutes, maybe less, before Jevan came down. He got into the car and told me to get under way quick and told me what had happened. We went to my house and sat out in front and decided what to do: just keep mum and lie if we had to——"

"As you did," said Wait.

Willy blinked. "Yes—well, I had to lie. You made me. I didn't want to be arrested myself. I didn't do it. Neither did Jevan. Or Dorcas."

"How do you know?" said Wait quietly.

"Because I—I know them."

"Look here, Devany, just why have you taken so active a hand in this thing?"

Willy's face flushed a little. "You mean the notice in the paper tonight. And—and coming here and all. Well, it's just as I told you. We—that is, Jevan and I didn't want you to know about Elise—didn't want anyone and especially Dorcas to know, for as Jevan said, sooner or later you would find some way to get the truth out of Dorcas and if she even knew of Elise you would take it to be a motive for her—Dorcas—wanting to murder Drew. Jevan said she'd be safer if she knew nothing of Elise. And then—after Marcus' murder we thought, of course, that Elise had done it. So we were trying to find her and find out what she knew (for if, after all she hadn't murdered Drew and convinced us she hadn't, it would only make things worse for Dorcas if you knew about

Elise). Jevan said the first thing to do was find Elise and talk to her. I thought of putting in the personal notice and did. It went like this . . ." He repeated it word for word. "I thought," he added naïvely, "that she would think 'W' meant Whipple and the whole thing meant money for her."

"Nine o'clock. Why weren't you here, then, when Mrs Locke got here?"

"Oh, that. Well, you see, somebody telephoned to my house and left a message from Jevan telling me to wait there for him and he might be late. So I waited and about nine, maybe a little after, he telephoned himself from the club where we'd originally agreed to meet. He said he hadn't left any message and that he was coming straight here. I said I would come, too, and he told me to wait downstairs. And I —I did," said Willy. "Till a couple of policemen came along and one of them recognized me and——"

"Who telephoned to your house the first time?"

"You mean who left the message, saying it was from Jevan? I don't know. Haven't any idea. No time to question the maid."

"But you and Locke did not come here together tonight? Did not even see each other until the police brought you up here?"

"N-no," said Willy. "That is, not since about noon."

"And for all you know it was Locke who telephoned your house in order to keep you away until he had met Elise and shot her?"

"No. Certainly not."

"You don't know," said Wait conclusively. "And you still haven't answered my question. Why have you so devoted yourself to your friends? To the extravagant point of being involved yourself in the murder."

"Involved," cried Willy, starting up and subsiding as abruptly. "I'm not involved in this. I only wanted to help Jevan if I could. And—and Dorcas."

Sophie's dark eyes held a queer look of scrutiny and she said suddenly: "He's always been in love with Dorcas, Mr Wait. Everybody's known it but Dorcas. He—why, he'd have murdered Ronald himself if he thought Ronald had— threatened Dorcas in any way. Not that he did," said Sophie. "But his efforts in Dorcas' behalf are perfectly comprehensible."

"Shut up, Sophie, for God's sake," cried Jevan. "I tell you, Wait, Willy's only an—an innocent bystander. You must believe me."

"Mrs Locke." Wait addressed Dorcas very softly, as if the thing he was about to say were of the smallest and most trivial significance. He said as she met his eyes: "There's a question you didn't answer, too, Mrs Locke. Remember? I asked you why Drew was afraid of your mother."

"Afraid——"

Jevan sprang to his feet.

"That's perfectly obvious," he cried. "You say that Marcus and Drew were conspirators—and perhaps they were. It sounds logical and true and the note—bears it out. Well then, if Drew said he was afraid of Dorcas' mother the explanation is perfectly simple. He was afraid that her influence upon my wife would destroy Drew's chances. Mrs Whipple was always against Drew and naturally he feared——"

"I expect that's true," said Wait. "Yes, I expect that's true, Locke. And that being true, I—I'm afraid there's only one thing I can do." He got up quietly, with the neat economy of motion of a cat. He looked at the table below his outstretched fingers for a moment that was all at once as quiet as if every pulse in that white and mirrored room had stopped. Instinctively Dorcas knew he had reached a decision. Jevan knew it too. His chin went up to face it like a man facing a firing squad. Willy twisted in his chair and stopped as if the little squeak of the chair might influence adversely that decision. Even Sophie was like a black, neat statue beside Dorcas but her hand, still on Dorcas' hand, held it rigidly.

Cary didn't do it, thought Dorcas numbly. Her little frail mother. It wasn't possible. But her heart was still and horribly heavy in her breast, as if laden with stones. And then Wait said quite gently: "I'm sorry, Locke."

"You——"

"I've considered it. And every consideration I put up— you knock down. And the—considerations," said Wait, clinging to the word, "were only tentative, an effort to see if any of them would bear the weight of investigation. But I did do that. I've been fair. But—my arrest has got to stand."

There was an utterly still moment. Dorcas could not look at Jevan. But she heard him say, breaking that stillness:

"The glass in the kitchen, the cigarette, Elise——"

"Elise was shot—she may die."

"But there are other things you haven't touched. Other"
—Jevan used the word too—"other considerations."

"Such as what?"

"The—the attempts to steal Marcus' reports."

Wait's eyebrows lifted. "Were there attempts to steal those
reports? Only a picture, hanging crooked."

"But the—the entrances into the house at night. The door
—the——"

Again Wait's eyebrows lifted.

"Nothing definite. Indeed, Locke, if those things mean
anything they mean that you arranged them deliberately in
an effort to indicate that someone outside was involved in
the thing. I've never taken those frequently and conveniently
opened doors and sundry presumable evidences of an intruder
prowling about the house very seriously. There's always been
something—well, something phony about it."

"But the door was left open," insisted Jevan, clinging desperately to a fighting chance. "Someone could have entered
the house——"

Wait shook his head. "Phony," he said. "It happened too
much. It was too obvious. It didn't," said Wait simply, "smell
right. . . . I'm sorry, Locke. But you were caught tonight
redhanded. And you are both under arrest."

"Both! You mean me——"

"If you are going to confess to save your wife, yes. But
it's my duty to arrest both of you. I—look here, Locke. I'm
not a man saying this. I'm just a—voice doing what it's here
to do. There'll be a trial and you have that chance." He
stopped. Willy muttered something and Sophie sighed and
leaned back against the divan and Wait called out: "O'Brien.
In here."

The door flung itself open as if O'Brien and the others
crowding behind him had read the meaning of that summons.

"I'm arresting Locke and his wife," said Wait. "Take them
to the station. Take them . . ." He hesitated and turned toward the door, saying over his shoulder, "Take them in my
car. No need to get a patrol wagon."

"Thanks, Wait," said Jevan and came to Dorcas' side. He
took her hands and pulled her to her feet and put his arms
around her. Warm and strong and gentle, and still he could
not really protect her except in an unthinkable way. She

clung to him, grateful for his nearness, overwhelmed by the cruel shock of recognizing futility. She knew she had not murdered Ronald, she knew by every deep-lying instinct in her that Jevan had not done it. Yet blindly, fatuously, they had walked into that net of evidence which now held them so securely there was no way out. Jevan's arms held her tightly. He whispered: "Dorcas—don't give up. The—the struggle hasn't begun. We'll get a good lawyer——"

She didn't know what else he said, for O'Brien was beside them. "If you please, Mrs Locke."

"You can't take her. I've confessed. I do confess. I——"

Wait's voice across the room was cool and grim: "Take them both, O'Brien."

"Never mind, Dorcas. They can't keep you long. They——"

"Hurry up, O'Brien."

"If you please, Mrs Locke. This way, Locke. You'll have to——"

Jevan's protecting arms were gone. A policeman was at Dorcas' elbow.

Willy was talking frantically, protesting. The mirrors and lights and voices were confusing. Sophie said harshly: "I'll have to go back and tell Cary. Here, Dorcas, get your hat on straight. You look like the wrath of God." She looked at Dorcas and from blind habit opened her black bag and glanced at her own haggard face in the little mirror and took out her lipstick. "I've got to go back and tell Cary," she repeated, applying lipstick with hands that shook and as if she were quite unconscious of what she was doing. "We'll get a good lawyer, Dorcas. We'll—but what will I tell Cary? It'll kill her."

Wait had turned around and was watching Sophie. "Cary . . ." he said. "Cary . . ."

Later Dorcas remembered the curious way the policeman's hand on her elbow seemed to stiffen. Then Wait went on, in exactly the same still, hushed way he had said, "Cary . . . Cary . . .": "O'Brien. Go downstairs. Get Mrs Whipple on the telephone. I'll talk to her down there."

O'Brien said, "Yes sir," very quickly and vanished. Wait looked at the remaining policemen and said: "Stay here. I'll be back shortly. Locke and Mrs Locke are under arrest. You know that. Devany, will you stay here, please. You, too, Mrs Whipple."

"What are you going to do?" demanded Jevan and Dorcas cried incoherently: "Not my mother. She knows nothing of this. She——"

Wait went out the door and one of the policemen said: "You heard his orders. Sit down if you want to. It won't be long. But you'd better not talk," he added hurriedly as Willy began to sputter unintelligibly about arrests and lawyers. He subsided, looking at Dorcas with worried eyes. Sophie closed her bag and touched her smart hat and sat erect on the edge of the sofa. And Dorcas met Jevan's eyes and was held by a look in them so deeply sustaining that it was as if he had taken her hands and made her a promise of the greatest possible significance. Yet—there was no way out. And Wait had gone to telephone to Cary—little, frail Cary. Cary, who had always been sheltered; Cary, who must be sheltered.

Cary, who had said childishly: "Promise to tell me, Dorcas, before they arrest you."

Mirrors all around them watched. And Wait came back.

Instantly Dorcas knew there was something different about him, something that had not been there when he went away. She couldn't have said in what subtle aspect he was different but she knew it and she said in a little gasp: "My mother——"

He gave her an absent glance. "We've got a little time to wait," he said to the room at large but chiefly to the policemen. "You may as well sit down, Mrs Locke. You, too, Locke. It ought not to be long. O'Brien."

"Yes sir."

"You'll see that Mrs Whipple is taken care of."

"Oh yes, sir. Certainly."

O'Brien turned around and went out the door. Dorcas' hands were clutching into the edge of the divan; she said hoarsely: "You mustn't bring my mother here. She had nothing to do with all this. It—It will kill her."

Wait, this time, looked at her consideringly for a moment before he replied. "You underestimate her strength and her intelligence. She—she saw you return, you know, the night Drew was murdered. She managed very cleverly not to tell me." He paused thoughtfully. Jevan was watching him with strained attention which had in it a tinge of knowledge. Did he know—did he guess—what was in the detective's mind? "I may as well tell you what happened while we wait," said the detective coolly. "Perhaps you can help me piece out the story——"

"*Story*," said Willy burstingly, with his eyes bulging. "What do you mean?"

Wait gave him a disapproving look. "Exactly what I say."

"But—but do you mean Mrs Whipple——"

"I'll tell you what I mean," said Wait. "And as I say, perhaps you can help."

"Me? But I——"

"Go on, Wait," said Jevan shortly.

Wait sat down, taking time to adjust himself comfortably, while Willy's eyes bulged and he ran a finger nervously around his collar.

"All right," said Wait. "There were some things I overlooked; some things that didn't quite balance and at least two things to which I failed completely to give proper weight. Now," he said simply, "I see that there had to be a third person in the scheme Drew and Pett had engaged upon. Neither man would have been at all likely to approach the other; Drew was not in any position to discover Pett's embezzlement, for he was in no way associated with him. Indeed, one of the salient points of the case was the fact that Drew and Pett were associated because of only one person and that was Dorcas Locke. That their orbits, so to speak, touched at only one point and that point was Mrs Locke. Mrs Locke and, naturally, the people closest to her. Also what I now see was a real attempt to steal Pett's reports later took place; it was a real attempt, not phony camouflage, because this third person realized that the instant Pett's embezzlement came to light the whole story would come out too. And thus almost inevitably the truth of the murder——"

"The murder of—Drew?" said Jevan.

"And of Pett. But the murder of Drew—listen." He paused, got up, prowled about the room for a moment and then said again: "Listen. You hear often of reconstructing the crime; let's do a little reconstructing here and now. On the scene of the murder. To begin with let's agree that the person in the kitchen was the murderer——"

"A woman," said Willy. "There's the lipstick on the cigarette——"

"Perhaps," said Wait briefly. "Listen. That person, impatient to know the outcome of Drew's last attempt to achieve their mutual end, has come to the apartment and entered, waiting in the kitchen, perhaps, trying to overhear. Drew naturally knows of it, having been in the kitchen to mix a

drink, and the realization spurs him on. But he fails and Mrs
Locke leaves. We've gone over this before. Well then. After
Mrs Locke's departure a quarrel takes place—each perhaps
accuses the other of not having done his part. They are both
bitterly disappointed, both perhaps have been drinking. In
the end, however, Drew realizes that he has lost everything.
And he . . ." He paused again, in deep thought. His voice
had taken on during the last moment or two a kind of
dreamy, musical quality; his eyes were almost mystic in their
dark opacity; actually he was only drawing conclusions from
results, adding well-recognized motives of human conduct
together to make a sum which he already knew. Working
backward slowly and ploddingly, yet with the sure tentacles
of imagination and insight. He took up the small, mirrored
cigarette box and looked into it dreamily as if it were a crystal ball and said: "Perhaps Drew demanded more money.
Perhaps he realized that of the three conspirators he was the
only one in actual need of money and that while both of the
others had not only sufficient money to live on but also possible ways to get more money from Dorcas Whipple he had
nothing. He had lost everything and thus had nothing more
to lose. But they—both of them still had something. Yes, I
think that's the way he would reason. I think in the end he
would say: 'Look here—give me more money or I'll tell
Dorcas Whipple the whole story. Make Pett dip into her fortune again for money for me or I'll tell her the whole dirty
scheme. I can't lose thereby, for I've already lost. But you
can lose the money and the opportunity to get more, that
you still have.' Yes, he must have said that, for he was a
stupid man. And it brought to its hearer instant, sharply clear
and inescapable realization of the truth. For the truth was
that Drew could not be permitted to live. So," said Wait,
looking into space, "he was not permitted to live. He was
shot then and there. . . ."

He stopped again. No one moved, perhaps no one
breathed.

It was as if the room itself had become at last articulate,
but articulate only to the sensitive ears of the man before
them. In a moment he continued more certainly now, as the
thing gained momentum. "Escape was easy. Locke came
along later and we know what he did. But almost at once another realization became clear to that third person and that
was that Pett was now a danger. For Pett balked at murder;

Pett must have guessed what had happened, though probably, cowardly, he dodged the truth. And in the end Pett's troublesome conscience got the better of him. He brought the reports which would show up his own embezzlement and thus certainly the conspiracy; for there were those checks to Drew to be accounted for. There was, as I say, the attempt to steal those reports and it failed. Pett was a danger. And then suddenly another danger developed and that was Elise—Drew's wife—who might be supposed to know something of the plot. And Elise actually came to the Whipple house. It was a mistake on her part.

"She may have come simply to tell of what she must know in an effort to discover her husband's murderer. She may have had a less admirable motive. Whatever her motive was (and we'll know if she recovers) she was frightened away. No one knew exactly when she left; she may have been in the house for some time. It happened by a not extraordinary combination of circumstances that every one of the little inner circle of people close to Dorcas Locke was at the Whipple house that afternoon. Thus any one of them might have done it."

"The green scarf . . ." It was Willy, white around the mouth and agitatedly twisting slender fingers, but still apparently helpful.

Wait's dark eyes shot briefly toward him: "Showing that that interview took place in the house—somewhere less public, certainly, than the room in which Elise was told to wait. The house was quiet at that hour; the interview was easy enough to arrange and Elise was frightened away. And then Marcus Pett came, ready to unburden himself and—had to be killed. Silenced then and there as Drew was silenced. With Drew it was his own revolver—he kept it in the drawer of this table." Wait touched the white table lightly. "Any of his acquaintances might have known it was there. With Pett it was a knife which, again, anyone long familiar with the Whipple house would have known where to find. And then next day Elise looms again as a danger. The police are trying to find her; Locke wants to find her; very well then, she must be found and silenced and the murderer must find her first. A personal notice appears in the paper——"

"I didn't kill Drew," cried Willy shrilly and Wait swerved around with an expression so suddenly savage that it seemed to check Willy, and repeated swiftly: "A personal notice appears which anyone may see and there's a slip-up in Locke's arrangements to come here. He is delayed and arrives later alone. And Elise mysteriously—how we may never know if she herself doesn't live to tell us—but with a ruthlessness typical of everything we know of the murderer, is shot——"

"Wait," broke in Jevan suddenly. "Wait, listen to me. You've left out motive. The obvious motive of money doesn't apply. You are all wrong——"

"Money?" repeated Wait. His eyes all at once became opaque again and dreamy. He shook his head slowly. "No, Locke, you're wrong. There's a motive as old as the world. And as mad and ugly and tragic as a life warped by it may be. And that motive," said Wait simply, "is jealousy. . . . And a jealousy, a deep, grudging jealousy, nourished for years only upon itself, which is the worse because of a necessity always to hide itself. To veil itself in friendliness and affection. Never to come out, to remain hidden like a cancer, destroying secretly——"

Jevan was standing, his face like granite. "You're all wrong, Wait! It's a twisted, unnatural motive you're suggesting. All this is only theory. You've no fact——"

"I have fact and I have proof. I have reason and logic. You've heard my reconstruction of the crime. Reason always needs facts as a basis; I had facts and I now also have the one key fact which links the others together. Circumstantial evidence," said Wait, "and identification."

Someone was coming up the stairs; there were footsteps and a murmur of voices in the corridor outside. Dorcas' heart was in her throat; she looked at the door and then jerked back toward Wait as he spoke again.

"Money," he said musically, two small rubies glowing deep in his eyes. "Money—and jealousy. Two of the simplest, strongest motives in the world. Mrs Locke, about a week ago you made a small purchase. After spending a lot of time on the subject I managed to trace it to you—the sales number appears on your charge account. At Field's this time. The record of that purchase if brought against you during a trial for murder would almost certainly convict you; it was, indeed, such important evidence that I intended to save it for the trial; to keep it a secret until we were ready to use it and thus take the defense by surprise. I could not, however, discover that object in your possession and until I talked to your mother just now I had no way of knowing what you had done with it. Now I know that it was your custom——"

The door opened.

O'Brien looked in and caught Wait's eyes and Wait stopped short and said: "All right."

O'Brien's face vanished. The policeman beside Dorcas, up to now a mute, rigid blue column, made a swift, barely perceptible movement and had a revolver in his hand and Cary Whipple came into the room. She was huddled in a fur coat and her blue eyes darted once around the room and fastened upon Wait, and a man followed her and stopped just beside her. Dorcas must have made some motion to go to her mother, for Jevan's hand gripped her own and held her near him, and Sophie, too, had risen.

But no one spoke. For a strange, sharp instant or two they were all as still as so many wooden people. Then Wait said: "Mrs Locke. Answer me quickly, please."

She tore her eyes from Cary to look at him. His voice was perhaps a little deeper than usual; otherwise she had no way of knowing how much he was staking upon her reply.

"Tell me what you did with the lipstick you bought at Field's shortly before your marriage."

"Lipstick?"

"Did you give it to anyone? As your mother says is your custom to give your dresses, suits——"

"I—don't——" But suddenly she did remember. A new tube of lipstick and she hadn't liked the shade of it and the night Ronald was killed . . .

That was as far as she got. For the man beside Cary leaned forward at once so his face jutted out into the light and he was the taxi driver; the first taxi driver; the one who had said Dorcas was not the woman he had brought to the Whipple house. He said now loudly: "That's the woman. That one over there. In black," he said and pointed at Sophie Whipple.

Dorcas always was to remember that. And she always was to remember the look in Sophie's eyes as if all the hatred and envy in the world were distilled therein and allowed for the first time to show itself, seething.

"*You*," said Sophie with dreadful, cold clearness. "You always had everything! And I nothing but what you chose to give me. Living on your charity, taking what you gave me, despising you all——"

"Take her away," said Wait.

It was long after midnight and the street before the Whipple house dark and quiet when a car came slowly to the gate and stopped. Willy drove it and Dorcas and Jevan were with him. Cary long ago had been brought back home.

Willy turned off the engine and they sat in silence, staring into the light lanes stretching ahead of them. Finally Willy sighed. "He must have recognized the lipstick the instant she took it out of her bag—he said he'd spent a lot of time having the lipstick analyzed that was on the cigarette she smoked in the kitchen."

"Obviously," said Jevan.

Dorcas said stiffly:

"But how did she dare come down in my green suit and show herself to the doorman and Wait?"

"It was no risk," said Jevan. "She hadn't been there, probably, often enough to be recognized; the doorman was new and she knew he hadn't seen her that night. It was perfectly safe for her and yet, paradoxically, the very fact that she did it made her seem utterly and completely guiltless. As if, if she'd been guilty, she wouldn't have dared."

"And there never was anybody breaking into the house," said Willy. "I suppose she figured the range of suspects was sort of limited and she'd better fix up something to indicate that there was somebody else in on the thing. Somebody outside. To divert suspicion, huh? A—a what-do-you-call-it expedient?"

"Sophie," said Jevan a little dryly, "was nothing if not —expedient."

Sophie, thought Dorcas, Sophie.

"But she really did try to get those reports. And Dorcas nearly caught her at it. And she made one slip when she left bloodstains on the towel after wiping the knife or washing her hands. She remembered later and washed the towel while the police were actually in the house. And calmly admitted it to Dorcas."

Willy gave an abrupt shiver. "Gosh! How could Sophie have killed Marcus! After all, you can't just walk up to a fellow and stick him with a knife. He—he stops you."

"You," said Jevan. "Or me. . . . Not a Sophie."

"If I'd known . . . if I'd guessed . . ." began Dorcas.

"Stop that, Dorcas. Sophie was what her nature made her. And she had to kill Ronald, for she thought if he told you the truth you would stop her allowance—and would be warned and armed against her. Sophie loved money, married for money, was bitterly disappointed when your father left her only a moderate sum which she ran through at once—murdered for it. Your money."

Willy said abruptly: "Well, I better be going on. . . ."

In the quiet, dark street Dorcas and Jevan watched the lights of his car recede and finally turn a corner, leaving the night altogether dark with, suddenly, stars. They turned and entered the gate. And in the shadow of it Jevan stopped and deliberately took Dorcas in his arms and put his mouth upon her own.

"I love you," he said and kissed her.

There was a long silence. The stars were clear and tranquil and his arms warm, holding her close. He said, whispering: "That annulment . . ." and waited.

She must have made some motion; her head, perhaps, against his heart, moved in negation. For he waited as if to be sure, there in the still darkness, and then said quite clearly: "Then—then you're my wife, Dorcas. To have and to hold. Against the world—in my arms—always."

After a while they turned slowly along the dark walk that led to the house.